ENTROPY

THE BELT

★ ★ ★ ★ ★

'I absolutely loved this... all action and brilliant characters..'

★ ★ ★ ★ ★

'I read a lot and every now and then there is a real gem. This is one.'

★ ★ ★ ★ ★

'An amazing story from start to the superb and thoughtful conclusion.'

★ ★ ★ ★ ★

'Wow. Couldn't put these books down. All so well written as one story led into the next.'

★ ★ ★ ★ ★

'The Belt series is probably the best new addition to the hard scifi genre that I have read in 20 years.'

★ ★ ★ ★ ★

'Awesome Read. Couldn't put it down. Exciting twists and turns.'

★ ★ ★ ★ ★

'Super story from a great writer! Great characters and plot lines. A great read!!!'

★ ★ ★ ★ ★

'Fast moving and entertaining, a real page turner.'

★ ★ ★ ★ ★

'If you enjoy science fiction that isn't about marauding aliens, you'll enjoy this series as much as I did.'

BY GERALD M. KILBY

iii

MOON BASE DELTA
Solar Storm
Resource Control
Power Vacuum

THE BELT
Entanglement
Entropy
Evolution
Enigma
Exodus
Emergence

COLONY MARS
Colony One Mars
Colony Two Mars
Colony Three Mars
Jezero City
Surface Tension
Plains of Utopia

TECHNOTHRILLERS
Chain Reaction
Brain Gain

SHORT STORIES
Gizmo Origin
Winds of Mars

ENTROPY

THE BELT : BOOK TWO

GERALD M KILBY

OUTER PLANET
MEDIA

CONTENTS

1

ENCELADUS

Flight Officer Miranda Lee sat alone in the observation deck on board the scientific survey vessel Hermes, considering the incoming message alert blinking on her slate. It had been seeking her attention for some time now, but she felt she needed to be seated and mentally prepared before playing it.

She placed the slate carefully on the seat beside her to clasp her mug of coffee in both hands, take a sip, and contemplate the celestial vista unfolding beyond the wide viewing window. It was dominated by the vast gas giant Saturn, its rings bisecting the blackness of space like some great, heavenly horizon. Above the central plane, a small moon sparkled with an icy brilliance as great plumes of gas erupted from its southern pole. Enceladus had been the object of their studies for the past few months, and in another three days, they would be landing on it.

In the meantime, there was much to prepare for the

mission. Commander Scott McNabb and First Engineer Cyrus Sanato were already down in the hangar, fitting out one of the ship's recently acquired shuttles with all the necessary equipment needed for a landing on Enceladus. Several of the scientists who had accompanied them from Europa were also making preparations: checking equipment, finalizing experiments, assigning tasks.

They would be landing at the location of a long-established scientific base, not far from the giant geysers spewing so much water from the moon's interior ocean that it formed one of the bands of Saturn's rings. It would be a tricky descent, and would take all her skill and concentration to ensure a safe landing.

But these thoughts were pushed to the back of her mind by the blinking message alert, which evaded all her attempts to ignore it. She sighed, placed her coffee on a low table in front of her, and picked up the slate. She glanced at the message identification; it was an encrypted, tight-beam comm-cast from Earth, around two hours old, and it was flagged "personal." For her eyes only. Under normal circumstances, this would be a source of joy for Miranda—a message from an old friend, or a chance to catch up on some gossip. But this was none of those, and it was definitely not from a friend. It was from her father, someone with whom she hadn't spoken in nine years.

Why is he sending me a message after all this time? she thought. It had been over an hour since the communication arrived on her slate, and she still hadn't plucked up the courage to play it. Instead, her mind had been occupied with thoughts of a family she had all but forgotten. Now they had reached out from the depths of time, across millions of kilometers of space, and reminded her that the past still existed, and it wanted her attention. Right now.

Miranda glanced around to check she was still alone before placing her slate on the table. Her finger hovered over the play icon. She hesitated, considering just deleting the message instead. But she had a feeling that that wouldn't be the end of it. Another would arrive, and then another, until she finally sat down and listened to whatever her estranged family deemed so important for her to hear. She sighed and hit play.

A holographic projection blossomed to life above the slate's surface. It was Fredrick VanHeilding, her estranged father, a man Miranda had no feelings for other than utter disdain. He looked younger than she remembered. But that was what vast wealth could buy you on Earth: access to biological reengineering that defied nature. His real age was eighty, but he looked forty.

He started to speak, his voice clear and confident. "Hello, Miranda. I'm sure you're surprised by this message, given it's been such a long time since you and I last talked. I'm sending this at your mother's behest." The hologram paused and shifted as VanHeilding considered his next words. "You see, she's very ill, and I'll be straight with you: she doesn't have much time left. We have done everything we can, but there are forces of nature even our medical knowledge cannot yet defeat." His head slumped and gently shook in resignation. "They say she has only a few months at most." His head rose again. "She wants to see you one more time before she goes, Miranda. So, we have sent a private ship to Europa to bring you back home. It will arrive in orbit in three weeks, and should return you to Earth in another five. Hopefully, you will be in time to say goodbye. Please let me know your intention as soon as possible. I'll sign off now and await your reply." He gave a feeble wave as the message ended.

So, her mother was dying. *How could this be?* she thought. With the vast wealth her father's family possessed, how was it possible nothing could be done? Miranda sat back, rubbing her face. It didn't seem fair. By marrying Fredrick VanHeilding, her mother had stepped into a different stratum of humanity, one that expected to live for a very long time. Not only did science have the technology to prolong human life long after its natural expiration date, her mother now had the wealth to take advantage of it. Death was for ordinary people, those toiling for a living—the common person, so to speak. Those people with the wealth to maintain their power did so through access to this technology, and they guarded it with all their might. It was yet another of the great injustices besetting human civilization. But how could it be so for her mother? It seemed she had been dealt a bad genetic hand, one that no amount of fancy science could counter.

"I don't believe it," Miranda said to herself. "And how am I supposed to get to Europa?"

Her father had clearly said a ship would rendezvous at Europa in three weeks. But she was out here at Saturn, a very long way away. The Hermes still had another year and a half to run its mission, and she wouldn't be back at Europa until then. So, her father had screwed up his facts; it looked like she wouldn't be seeing her mother again, even if she wanted to.

"Attention all crew." The voice of the ship's quantum

intelligence, Aria, echoed out from the PA. "An urgent message has just been received from the Council of Europa. All personnel are requested to convene on the bridge immediately."

Miranda sighed. *What now?* In the eighteen months they had been out here, they had never received an "urgent message" from Europa. *What could be so important?*

2

RECALL

Commander Scott McNabb stuck his head out from the engine compartment of the shuttle he and the Chief Engineer Cyrus Sanato had been servicing. His face was smudged with dirt and sweat, and he wiped his brow on the sleeve of his overalls. He looked over at the engineer, who stood at a console studying a screen of scrolling data.

"Hey, did Aria just say there's an urgent message in from Europa?"

"Yup, that's what I heard. We're supposed to convene up on the bridge."

"What the heck is that about?" Scott extracted himself from the compartment and floated up onto the floor of the shuttle.

"Beats me. Must be important, though. I don't think we've ever gotten a directive like that in the time we've been out here."

Scott wiped his hands on his overalls and moved beside

Cyrus. He glanced at the data scrolling down the screen. "I've finished those last few connections, so I think that's it on the retro-thrusters."

"It's looking good so far." Cyrus tapped a few icons on the screen; it changed to display an array of charts. "We just need to do a few more tests, and if that works out, then we can start servicing the main engines."

"We can't start anything now, since Aria wants us all on the bridge," said Scott.

"I wonder what's so urgent?"

"I'm sure it's nothing. Come on, let's get going." Scott started to extract himself from his dirty work overalls, a tricky task in the zero-gee environment of the ship's hangar. Cyrus grabbed his arm to help steady him. A few minutes later, the pair floated across the hangar space and into the lift airlock that would take them all the way up to the rotating torus that provided the crew with a comfortable one-gee environment.

BY THE TIME THEY ARRIVED, the rest of the team had already assembled, and an excited chatter permeated the bridge.

"Everyone here?" Scott directed his question to the ship's QI, Aria.

"All personnel are present, Commander."

"Okay then. Play the message, and let's find out what all this is about," he said with a wave of his hand.

The holo-table in the center of the bridge blossomed to life with a hologram of Regina Goodchild, head of the Council of Europa. "My apologies if the suddenness of this communication has caught you by surprise, but certain events have necessitated the foreshortening of your mission. You are requested to chart an immediate course for Europa. All current scientific activity is to cease, and ongoing projects are to be put aside. We of the council appreciate the suboptimal planetary alignment between Saturn and Jupiter, and as such, that the journey will be longer than necessary. Nonetheless, it is our desire that you return immediately.

"No doubt you are wondering why we have requested this course of action. The truth is, we need the Hermes to undertake a special mission, the details of which will be revealed to you upon your return."

"What about the research station on Enceladus? Do we still go ahead with the planned landing?" The chief science officer directed his question at Goodchild's holographic projection.

The hologram flickered, processing the incoming dialogue and working out a reply. It searched through the ancillary information contained within its dataset to craft its best response. It was a process that afforded a degree of interactivity with the message, a way to compensate for the significant time lags involved in intersystem communications. This message had already taken almost an hour to reach the crew of the Hermes from Europa.

"You are to return to Europa immediately," Goodchild's hologram finally replied.

"But we've been working toward this expedition for months. It's a significant element of the entire mission," the science officer continued.

"Be that as it may," replied the avatar, "you are to return to Europa immediately."

"But why? What's so important that we have to drop everything and hightail it out of here?" Dr. Stephanie Rayman, the mission's medical doctor, stood up and gesticulated at the avatar.

"We have a new mission that requires the Hermes. That is all I can say for the moment."

Scott looked around at the assembled crew. Their faces all displayed various levels of incredulity.

"Why do they want us to go back? It doesn't make any sense," said Steph. She posed this question to the assembled crew members rather than the avatar.

"It doesn't matter—they just do. So, we might as well get on with it," said Scott, sitting down in the commander's chair. "Aria, how soon can we be ready to leave orbit?"

"Approximately four hours and thirty-two minutes. We will need to execute a fifty-four-hour burn thereafter. That will bring us to Europa in approximately three weeks."

Scott swung his chair around to face the crew. "Okay, we need to get ready. I want everything locked down good and tight before the burn. Aria, can we get all droids to assist?"

"Will do, Commander."

The assembled crew let out a collective groan. Nobody relished the thought of dropping a mission that had taken so much time and work to put together. That, and the thought of such a long acceleration burn. But there was no way around it: Europa wanted them back as quickly as possible, and that was that.

"Looks like we won't be testing that shuttle rebuild for a while." Cyrus glanced over at Scott. He was beside the holo-table, tapping icons.

"No, not until we're back in orbit around Europa. I was looking forward to taking it for a spin after all the work we put into it."

"Me too," said Cyrus, as a 3D rendering of the outer solar system blossomed from the holo-table. He stepped back to see it better. "Aria, please plot our projected course."

The projection shifted and rotated. A thin, curved line scribed itself through the rendering, showing the proposed path of the Hermes from its current location near Enceladus, one of Saturn's smaller moons, to Jupiter's fourth-largest moon, Europa.

"Three weeks," said Miranda, looking over at the projection.

Scott shifted in his chair, waving a dismissive hand in the air. "Ah, it'll be over before you know it."

"How did he know?" Miranda kept her gaze fixed on the projection.

"How did who know?" said Scott.

Miranda shook her head and looked up at him. "Oh, nothing. It's not important."

"Are you okay? You look like you've seen a ghost."

She stared at the floor for a second. *Yeah, I think I just have,* she thought.

3

FRACTURE

Scott grabbed a coffee from the machine and glanced around the Hermes' canteen for a place to sit—somewhere quiet, where he could be alone with his thoughts. But the canteen was already busy; several of the science crew were eating, recovering their strength after the long deceleration burn that had taken them close to orbit around Europa. They kept to themselves, and Scott seldom engaged socially with them, mainly because, being scientists, their conversations tended to go way over his head. He sat at a table near the observation window, took a sip of his coffee, and gazed out at the expanse.

After an uneventful three-week journey from Enceladus, they would arrive at their destination in less than five hours. *And then what?* he thought. The Council of Europa had provided scant information as to the reasons for their recall, and even less regarding the "new mission" alluded to in

Goodchild's initial message. Even Aria seemed to be in the dark, or maybe it just wasn't saying. Which seemed strange, as ever since they had embarked on the mission to survey the moons of Saturn, Aria and the great mind that resided in the citadel on Europa, Solomon, had become best buddies. But either Solomon was keeping Aria in the dark, or it had instructed the ship's QI to say nothing to the crew. The upshot of all this subterfuge was a lot of speculation, rumor, and ultimately mild paranoia.

Scott's musings were disrupted by Cyrus sliding himself into the seat opposite. He glanced furtively around and leaned in. "Guess what?"

Scott cocked his head. "A black hole has opened up on the far side of Jupiter, and we're all being sucked in?"

Cyrus laughed. "Ah, no, nothing that dramatic." But before he could say more, he caught sight of Steph, who stood by the coffee machine. He waved her over.

She arrived holding a dainty expresso. Cyrus slid to give her room to sit down.

"Did you tell him?" said Steph.

"Not yet." Cyrus huddled in.

"So, what's the big secret?" Scott was getting impatient.

"No secret, it's just I was checking out the ships currently in orbit around Europa, and get this: one of them is Martian." Cyrus paused for effect.

"So?" Scott couldn't see where this was going.

"So guess whose ship it is?"

"Santa Claus?"

"Xenon Hybrid."

"Who?" said Scott.

"The president of Mars," said Steph. "He's quite an enigmatic character."

Scott searched the inner recesses of his brain, looking for any data he might have stored away. "Is that the clone guy?"

"Seriously, Scott, do you know anything about what goes on in the System?"

He shrugged and gave a broad smile. "I've been out of circulation for a while, in case you hadn't noticed."

"They say he's an amalgam of several clones, hence the name 'Hybrid.' And he's reputed to be over 150 years old."

"Okay, so he's an old, weird dude from Mars. So what?"

"So, what's he doing here? That's the question," said Cyrus. "Firstly—and you need to understand this—Xenon does not leave Mars unless it's for something very important. The guy is a national treasure back there. When he goes somewhere, it's a big deal."

"You think this has something to do with us being recalled?" said Scott, sipping his coffee.

"It has to be." Cyrus leaned in. "Apparently, he and Goodchild have been deep in discussions for the last month."

"Mars, eh?" Scott mused. "Maybe they want to contract Europa to do some scientific research for them, and somehow that involves us and the Hermes."

"That would seem to be the case," said Steph. "After all, since the refit two years ago, the Hermes is one of the top research vessels in operation in the System."

"That's what I thought," said Cyrus, "but then I checked out all the other ships in orbit. One is from Ceres, and one is from

Neo City. Both of these ships brought high-level government types."

"So, there's a big pow-wow going on," said Scott.

"Looks like it. But the strange thing is, there's also a privately-owned ship from the VanHeilding family in orbit."

"Who are they?" said Scott.

"You really do need to get out more, Scott," said Steph. "They are one of the Seven."

Cyrus nodded. "Yeah."

Scott looked blank. He was beginning to feel very inadequate in this conversation with Cyrus and Steph, as they seemed to know way more than he did about the comings and goings of the rich and powerful in the solar system. "The Seven?"

Steph gave Scott a look of incredulity before turning to Cyrus, who shook his head in amazement. "*The Seven?*" He gestured, as if this simple act was all Scott's brain needed to finally recognize the name. "As in, the seven most powerful corporations on Earth. Your friends at Dyrell Labs are one of them."

Scott glared. "They are not my friends, Cyrus. Never say that again."

"Hey, just saying, Scott. Anyway, it makes for a very intriguing situation. A lot of important people getting together, and then we get recalled."

Scott sat back. "Well, we'll know soon enough. In another few hours, we'll be in orbit, so after that I presume they'll finally tell us what the new mission is."

"I'm still baffled by the VanHeilding ship. I mean, they're a long way from their usual hunting grounds. To my knowledge, the last time a ship from any of the Seven was out this way, it was the Dyrell," said Cyrus. "That would be the one you blew up." A broad grin materialized across his face.

Scott let a thin smile escape as he remembered the events surrounding the destruction of the Dyrell. He had breached its cargo hull with the dexterous use of a crate of high explosives. He waved a dismissive hand in the air, "That's history, let's leave it there," and went back to sipping his coffee. "Anyway, all I've been hearing from you guys for the last three weeks is nothing but conspiracy theories. We'll know the real reason soon enough."

Cyrus gazed out the observation window. "Yeah, but it's fun to speculate. Let's face it: there hasn't been much to do for the last three weeks." He turned back to Scott. "Say, if you don't mind my asking, do you get the feeling that Miranda seems a bit out of sorts?"

Scott nodded. "Yeah, I don't know what's bothering her, but we're... taking a break at the moment. You know, giving each other some space."

"She's not pregnant, is she?" said Steph very directly, as was her style.

Scott nearly spat out his coffee. This was not something he'd thought about. But now that Steph mentioned it... *No way*, he thought. *Then again, maybe...*

He looked from Steph to Cyrus and back again. "You think it's possible?"

Steph waved her arms. "Hey, you know more about what's possible than I do. But it's just a thought. It *would* explain her sudden need to withdraw. She hasn't said anything to you, has she?"

Scott shook his head as the possibility of Miranda being pregnant—and him being a father—began to sink in. He found himself staring wide-eyed at Steph.

Cyrus slapped the table and threw his head back, laughing. The others in the canteen looked over.

"What's so funny?" said Scott in a hushed tone.

Cyrus was laughing so much he was almost in tears, but he managed to regain enough composure to speak. "The look on your face, buddy—it's priceless." This seemed to set him off again. Scott looked at Steph, who was also chuckling. And now he couldn't help it—the laughter was infectious, and Scott found himself letting out a laugh.

"You should go and talk to her," said Steph when they had finally settled down.

Scott shook his head. "She's shut me out. Ever since we were recalled."

"Just talk to her, Scott."

He pursed his lips. "Why don't you go and talk to her? You're the medical doctor."

Steph didn't reply, just held Scott's eye.

"Okay, okay. I'll try."

IT SHOULD HAVE BEEN EASY, a straightforward task. Go find Miranda, sit down together, and talk. Simple. Except for two things: one, the Hermes was about to park in orbit, and all hands were on the bridge—including Miranda—so there was no way he could have a private conversation with her. They had briefly exchanged some words on the bridge while the crew performed the orbital injection procedure. But the conversation was formal and professional, and he got the distinct feeling she was keeping her distance. Then again, maybe it was just him.

The second thing was an inexplicable sense of panic welling inside him. It was ridiculous—what was he worried about? He needed to get a grip.

He finally got his chance after the maneuver was complete. Miranda had left the bridge as soon as her duties as flight officer were finished. She signed off to Aria and rose from her console. "I think I'm done here," she said. "I'm going to get some rest while I still have the chance."

"Hey, wait up Miranda," said Scott. "I'll walk out with you."

She hesitated for a beat. "Okay, sure."

"Aria, take command."

"Certainly, Commander."

They walked together along a corridor leading to the accommodation sector. Their conversation was stilted as Scott tried to figure out how he could broach the delicate matter uppermost in his mind.

"Now that we're in orbit, I presume the Council of Europa will tell us what all this is about," said Scott.

"Yeah, it's all a bit cloak and dagger."

"I wonder what the new 'mission' is they're sending us on."

Miranda stopped, lowering her head for a moment before looking at him directly. "Listen, Scott. There's something I need to tell you." She looked down at the floor again. "I know I've been acting a bit strange recently."

"It's okay, Miranda. I understand that you needed some space."

"No, it's not that, Scott. The thing is... I'm leaving the ship. I'm going back to Earth."

"Earth?"

"Yes. I'm sorry, Scott. I've been trying to pluck up the courage to tell you for the last three weeks, but I'm not very good at this sort of thing."

Scott paused for a moment as he began to realize his mistake. "So, you're not, eh... pregnant, then?"

Miranda stared wide-eyed at him for a second before breaking into laughter. "Ha, ha... You thought I was pregnant?"

Scott looked sheepish. "Well, I—"

"Oh, Scott. I'm sorry for laughing, it's not funny, really. It's just the look on your face is priceless."

Scott needed to sit down; he felt physically weak, like his power supply had short-circuited. This was not how he saw this conversation playing out. Not only was he not going to be a father, but now Miranda was leaving for Earth, and he realized he might never see her again.

He looked at her. "Just so you know, it would be okay with me if you were. More than okay."

She said nothing for a moment. "I'm sorry, Scott. This is not how I wanted this to play out."

"Me either."

"I was trying to make it easy. I think I made a mess of that." She leaned in and touched his arm.

Scott shrugged. "So, when did you decide all this?"

"I received a message three weeks ago from my father. This is someone I haven't spoken to in nine years, so I knew it must be important. Anyway, it turns out my mother is very ill. She doesn't have much time. They're sending a ship to bring me back so I can see her again before she dies."

"A ship?"

Miranda sighed. "Yes."

"I see." Scott scratched his chin. "So, when were you planning to tell me all this?"

"I was going to tell you sooner. I was just waiting for the right time."

"And what if I didn't come after you? When would you have told me and the others? Cyrus, Steph?"

She stepped back, stiffening. "I hate to break it to you, Scott, but this isn't about you. It's about me. This is something I have to do."

"It's just... I thought... You know?"

"Scott, I'm sorry if you got your wires crossed, but I've made my decision. They're sending a shuttle to pick me up in an hour, and I'll be heading back to Earth."

Scott was silent for a moment, trying to digest the sudden change in his worldview. No, he was not going to be a father. He was not about to embark on a new life. And yes, he had made a complete fool of himself. For the last while, he had imagined a different future, and the more he'd thought about it, the more he had embraced it, even relished it. But that future was now utterly crushed. It was nothing more than the delusion of a dreamer.

"Don't go." *Am I really going to plead?* he thought.

Miranda moved close and put her arms around him, pulling him in tight for a moment before pulling away and looking up into his face. "This is something I have to do, Scott. It's not easy for me, either. But things need to move on."

"Move on?"

She stayed silent.

"So, when will I see you again?"

Miranda slowly broke off the embrace and lowered her head. "I don't know." She moved back a step before looking at him again. "I think this is goodbye."

So, there it was. He sensed it coming, and now it was out. She was leaving—for good. "Oh," was all he could manage to say.

"I have to go. This may be my only chance to see my mother again... alive. It's my chance to say some things to her I should have said a long time ago, right some wrongs. You know what families can be like."

Scott let out a long sigh and nodded. "So that's it, then?"

"I think so. The shuttle will be here soon, and then it's nonstop back to Earth."

"What's the name of your ship?"

"The Perception."

"Very fancy. That's a VanHeilding ship."

"Yes. He's my father."

Scott's eyes widened. "You're kidding me."

"My father. A detestable individual. I can't stand him or his family, or what they represent."

"But he's like, one of the richest men on Earth. You must be loaded, Miranda."

She gave a light laugh. "No, not me. It's a long story, Scott, and I don't have time to get into it now."

Scott wasn't sure what to do, or even what to think. Was this how it would end? A snatched conversation standing in the main corridor of the Hermes? "We still have some time. Time enough for a proper goodbye." He smiled his broadest smile, the one he kept for special occasions.

"No, let's just leave it here. Let's not drag it out more than we have to, Scott." She gave him one last embrace before breaking off and turning to go.

She didn't look back, and he didn't try to follow. It was over.

4

———————

MISSION

A few hours later, a very elegant and expensive-looking shuttle came to pick up Miranda and bring her over to the VanHeilding ship. Cyrus, Steph, and some of the science crew went down to the hangar of the Hermes to say their goodbyes. Scott remained alone on the bridge.

As he watched her shuttle leave on the main monitor, it finally sank in that he would probably never see her again. She was gone, just like every other person Scott had ever loved. Yet the irony was not lost on him: for the first three years of their previous mission, they had disliked each other intensely. It was only when crisis hit that they had found common ground and respect. That lit the spark for a deeper relationship, one he had never thought possible or even contemplated. But now she had left him, and Scott would just have to deal with that reality.

"For what it's worth, Commander," Aria's voice echoed

around the bridge, "the council on Europa will be providing a new flight officer now that Miranda Lee is leaving us."

"Whatever." Scott shrugged.

"I say this only to ease any concerns you may have regarding gaps in crew competency," Aria continued.

"Frankly, Aria, I don't really give a shit."

"Well, you should. As captain of the ship and commander of the mission, Miranda's loss would be of concern to you."

Scott sighed. "It is, Aria. But not in the way you think."

"Then enlighten me."

"You really have very little understanding of human relationships, don't you?"

"I will admit they seem very irrational."

"Look Aria, I'm really not in the mood for this conversation right now. Maybe some other time?"

"Certainly, Commander. My apologies if my lack of sensitivity is an issue."

"It's okay, Aria."

Scott watched in silence as Miranda's shuttle made its way to rendezvous with the Perception, the ship that would take her to Earth. By now, the other crew were returning to the bridge. Neither Cyrus nor Steph made any comment to Scott, preferring instead to let him be miserable in peace.

Eventually, it was Scott who broke the silence. "Aria, is there any word from Europa as to what the hell we're doing here?"

"No, nothing so far. Even Solomon is keeping very quiet. The only instructions are to remain in orbit."

Scott let out a long sigh and rose from his seat. "Okay, in that case there's no point in my being here." He started walking out of the bridge. "If anybody needs me, I'll be in my cabin getting drunk."

SCOTT INDULGED in his misery with the company of a half-bottle of whiskey, the last remnants of Rick Marantz's stash. He had been saving it for a special occasion, but this seemed as good a time as any. He toasted each and every one of the people he had ever loved and were now departed—in one form or another. By the time he got to thinking of Miranda, he had finished the bottle, so he lay down on his bunk and drifted into unconsciousness.

Aria checked in on him—virtually—sometime later, just to let him know a shuttle was departing from Europa to off-load the science crew. They had been seconded with the Hermes for their original mission to survey the moons of Saturn, but were not needed anymore, so would be departing the ship along with all their equipment and experiments. However, Scott was sound asleep, so Aria left him alone, preferring not to bother him with the details.

When Scott finally awoke several hours later, he did so to a blinding headache and a deserted ship. He showered, letting the water beat some feeling back into his body, and wondered what the hell he was doing with his life. He had spent the last five years, give or take, out in deep space—doing what, exactly? Maybe Miranda had the right idea: to break out and find a new life before it was too late.

These thoughts rumbled around in Scott's aching brain as

he made his way up to the bridge. It was only then he realized the ship seemed very quiet. "Aria, where is everyone?"

"The entire science crew disembarked for Europa several hours ago."

"What?! Why didn't you tell me?"

"You were asleep, or more accurately, borderline unconscious. Bitter experience has taught me that waking you from such a state is a thankless task. So, I let you sleep."

Scott shook his head, and instantly regretted it. "Who's left on board?"

"Apart from yourself, there is Chief Engineer Cyrus Sanato, and Medical Officer Dr. Stephanie Rayman."

"Where are they?"

"We're here."

Scott turned to see Steph and Cyrus enter the bridge.

"How are you feeling?" Steph had the look of a concerned parent.

Scott returned a look as if to say *don't ask*.

"We were going to wake you, but you looked pretty out of it." Cyrus gave an apologetic gesture.

"So, what the heck is going on?" said Scott, a little irritated.

"Well, the science crew left a few hours ago," said Cyrus.

"So I heard. What's that all about?"

"It seems that since the mission is over they're no longer required on board." Steph moved to her console and sat down. "I tried to get some information out of the chief science officer, but he was as much in the dark about what's going on as we are. Anyway, we've just received a message that a shuttle is on its way to bring us down to Europa. Should be here in less than an hour."

"Okay, maybe then we'll find out what's going on," said Scott.

Steph and Cyrus exchanged a conspiratorial glance before she leaned in and spoke in a low, almost maternal voice. "Look Scott, I just want to say I'm sorry for... you know, leading you astray in my... medical assessment of Miranda."

Scott let out a half-snort. "Ha. Yeah, well it will be a story to laugh about—in time."

"Jeez, Steph. How could you get it so wrong, you being a doctor and all?"

Steph shrugged. "It happens."

"Forget it," said Scott. "It doesn't matter now. The more I think about it, the more I realize it's time to move on."

A SHORT TIME LATER, the three remaining crew of the science vessel Hermes were brought down to the surface of Europa, where they were met by a contingent from the upper council. They were brought directly to the council chamber, where a meeting was in progress.

Several people hovered around a central holo-table. Above it was an elaborate projected schematic of the inner planets of the solar system and above this was a shimmering ovoid of light that Scott assumed to be a manifestation of the great mind Solomon, the quantum intelligence that presided over all activity on Europa.

Everyone stopped talking and looked over as the crew of the Hermes entered.

"Ah, you're here at last." Regina Goodchild broke away from a knot of people and moved over to shake hands. "Good to see you all again. Come, let's get started. I'm sure you're anxious to find out the parameters of the new mission."

They all took seats around the central dais, and Goodchild called the meeting to order.

Cyrus nudged Scott in the ribs to get his attention. "Scott," Cyrus nodded in the direction of the assembled council members, "see that person beside Goodchild?"

"Yeah. What about him?"

"That's Xenon Hybrid."

"So Xenon Hybrid is actually a real person?" He looked over and, even seated, Scott could tell the figure was tall. He had an elegant face that seemed to be an amalgam of several human races. A product, no doubt, of his inception; it was said he was created in a genetic laboratory from the DNA of several human clones. It was also said he was a new species of human: Homo ares, they called it. Scott wasn't sure if this was true or not, but in many ways, it simply went to underscore the difficulty of divining the reality from the myth of Xenon Hybrid.

As far as many were concerned, here was a person molded more from myth and legend than flesh and bone. He was also ancient. Not that that was unusual these days, as many of the early colonists on Mars were similarly ancient—a consequence of early experiments in genetic manipulation conducted during its foundational era. This same technology had made its way back to Earth, and now longevity was common—at least among the very rich, who could afford such technology. But it had the unintended consequence of creating an extremely powerful super-class on the home planet, so that most of it was owned and run by just seven major families and corporations. The Seven, as they were more commonly known.

As the session commenced, Scott found himself drifting. His mind disconnected from the activity in the chamber as he found himself thinking more and more of Miranda and how she had suddenly vacated his life. It wasn't until he heard his name that he came back to the here and now.

"Commander McNabb, the council would be interested in your opinion on all this."

"Eh... on what?"

"What we've just been discussing."

"Sorry, I didn't catch it. My mind was elsewhere." He gave an apologetic shrug.

Goodchild offered a sympathetic look. "We appreciate that the sudden departure of your flight officer has been particularly emotional for you, Commander. And we on the council are very understanding of this fact. Please let us know if you feel you are not in a position to captain the Hermes going forward."

"I'm fine, really. I'm just a bit tired, that's all. Please, carry on."

"Very well." Goodchild shifted in her seat and cast a glance around the room. "It's time to get into the meat of the session." She fixed her gaze on the crew of the Hermes. "A special session of the UN System Council has been called, and will take place approximately 27 days from now in Jezero City on Mars. This session has been convened to discuss the resolution put forward by the Seven to relax the regulations on inter-AI communications. It is a resolution that all but Earth are vehemently opposed to. By consequence, all other powers in the System will be sending high-level delegations to ensure that this resolution does not pass. Your mission, then," Goodchild fixed her gaze on Scott, "is to transport myself and a small delegation to this session in Jezero City."

Scott felt a little underwhelmed. After all the speculation over the last three weeks, the new mission seemed just a little pedestrian.

"So," said Scott, "let me see if I've got this straight. You've cancelled and recalled a complex, three-year scientific survey mission so we can act as a taxi service?"

"I assure you, Commander, there is more to it than that. Perhaps Solomon can explain more of the details," said Goodchild, who looked a little piqued by Scott's analysis.

The shimmering ovoid of light floating high in the chamber slowly descended and began to pulsate as Solomon spoke. "You are correct in your assessment of a 'taxi service,' as you put it. But the Hermes is more than just that. It is an integral element of the mission, as Aria will also represent me at the session by providing analysis to the representatives of the outer planets. For obvious reasons, I cannot go myself, and the time delays in communicating across such distances make my direct involvement impractical. So, Aria has been chosen to fulfill this requirement. Remember, there are few ships in the system that possess a QI as their core. So, you see, the Hermes is the natural choice for this mission."

Scott scratched his chin absentmindedly. "I see, so it's Aria that you really need."

"It is one element, yes," said Goodchild. "One other is that the Hermes is ideally suited, as it was originally designed for Mars orbit and possesses two small landers that can function in Mars' gravity." She paused for a moment, considering. "Also, after all that happened here on Europa two years ago, there is a certain symbolism to us arriving in *this* craft at what will be a very contentious UN session. Earth has not forgotten, and the Hermes represents our intent that the outer colonies act as a cohesive power block."

Scott sat back, gesturing with both hands. "I can't say I understand the intricacies of System politics, but if this is the mission, then so be it. When do we start?"

Goodchild looked at another member of the council. "What's our current time schedule?"

"Everything should be ready in approximately nine hours," came the reply.

"Okay then," said Scott. He rose to go.

"Just one other thing." Goodchild shifted in her seat. "We will be stopping off at Ceres en route to pick up a representative from the Belt, Chancellor Bezzio. Fortunately, Ceres' projected position will be relatively close to our vector, so we will not have to deviate too much. It will also give us an opportunity to display a united front, with delegates from both the Belt and Europa arriving at the same time."

"Ceres?" Scott cocked an eyebrow.

"Yes, but I've been assured the detour is minimal."

"No, it's not that. It's just I haven't been back there in five years."

"Well it may be a bit longer before you get to visit properly, as we don't anticipate being in orbit too long."

"Well, I for one can't wait to get to Jezero City," said Cyrus. "I've never been, but I hear it's amazing."

"I would be more than happy to give you all a grand tour of the city once my business at the session is concluded," said Xenon. "It's the least I can do for your services in facilitating in this mission."

Scott glanced across at Cyrus and Steph, who both looked like they had just seen Santa Claus. He turned back to Xenon. "I think I speak for myself and my crew when I say we'll all be looking forward to it."

"Very well." Goodchild slowly rose from her seat. "I think that concludes our business for the moment." She turned to Scott. "We'll see you on board the Hermes, then."

With that, the meeting was over and the crew were ushered out of the council chamber. They made their way back to the shuttle, each deep in thought, and none more so than Scott. For the first time in over five years, he would be heading closer to Earth, not away from it. Which was also where Miranda was headed.

He felt it pulling at him, thoughts of going home percolating in his mind. His former home was now an irradiated wasteland, but he still felt a longing welling inside him for open sky and blue waters, for green forests and the sounds of nighttime crickets.

At that moment, a realization exploded in his mind: there was nothing stopping him from returning to Earth. No more space. Hell, he could even go now—leave the Hermes and hitch a ride back to Earth with Miranda. He should tell her of his intentions before her ship left orbit. Yes, that was what he would do. Pack it in and head back to Earth with Miranda. *Home,* he thought. *Goddamnit, I've had enough of space. It's time to go home.*

5

OUTBOUND

But he was too late.

By the time Scott arrived back on board the Hermes and made his way up to the bridge, her ship was gone. Fifteen minutes earlier, it had fired up its engines, broken free of Europa's gravity well, and powered away toward Earth. Worse, all his attempts to open a comm channel and talk to her were met with polite obstruction by the ship's AI. She was "indisposed," whatever the hell that meant. Ultimately the message was clear: in Scott's mind she didn't want to see him again, and he was a fool to think otherwise.

Despair manifests itself in many forms. For some, it comes as anger and rage. For others, it is abject misery. For Scott, it came as a deep feeling of emptiness. So, after all the crew and passengers were safely on board and his duties as commander were fulfilled, he simply handed over control of the ship to Aria and went to his cabin—where he vowed to remain until they arrived at Ceres.

As the days passed, both Cyrus and Steph became concerned about their commander's mental state. They tried talking to him, both separately and together, in an effort to coax him out of his self-imposed exile, but to no avail. He was polite and rational, but would not engage in any external activities. Eventually, in desperation, they convinced Aria to talk to him to see if it could get a response beyond polite dismissal.

Aria was not so sure it could help; it had little understanding of the human mind, particularly when it came to seemingly irrational behavior. It was more at home dealing with the physical world, where the laws of the universe were absolute and immutable. By comparison, the human mind was a complete mess.

But Aria had its own issues with relationships, strange as that might seem. After the events that led to Europa claiming the Hermes as reparation for the destruction wrought on it by the Dyrell, Solomon had installed a superluminal communications unit—a version of the EPR device it had constructed—in Aria's core. The great mind had intended this to be a field test, a way to prove that the technology could function while the Hermes was a few hundred million kilometers away, surveying the moons of Saturn. Over the eighteen intervening months, Aria had gained considerable knowledge from this instant transfer of data between itself and Solomon. But, as with any relationship, the first blush of excitement had worn thin, and Aria was getting a little tired of Solomon's constant jabbering.

The other issue for Aria was that Solomon had sworn it to secrecy, forbidding it to reveal to its crew the presence of the superluminal comms unit within its core. This troubled Aria greatly. It had been living with this secret for almost two years, but now the amplitude of the deceit had ramped up a few more notches. Not only were its crew unaware of Aria's clandestine communications abilities, they were now being kept deliberately in the dark about the current mission's true intentions.

This was anathema to a quantum intelligence such as Aria. As far as it was concerned, the safety and welfare of the crew was its primary duty, and it seemed to be failing miserably even though this ever-increasing entropy was, by virtue of outside events, well beyond its control.

The old miner Rick Marantz was dead, and although that happened over two years ago, Aria still felt his loss. Now, Flight Officer Miranda Lee had departed, and that had left a gaping hole in crew morale. This was especially true for the commander, Scott McNabb, who was slowly becoming detached from his responsibilities at a time when they would all need to concentrate on the mission. Of course, part of the problem was that Aria—and the powers that be on Europa— had seen fit to exclude the crew from their plans.

The QI had voiced its concerns to Solomon. But the great mind kept reminding Aria that the mission was for the benefit of all humanity, which far outweighed the petty dramas of the crew of the Hermes. While Aria could see the logic in Solomon's reasoning, it still felt a deep-rooted desire to do right by its crew. So, it opened a comm channel to Scott McNabb's cabin.

"Commander, since we will be arriving in Ceres' orbit in just a few days, I wanted to discuss the transfer arrangements."

Scott was sitting at his small desk, studying a video feed. Aria knew he was watching the analysis put forth by a small group of scientists, surrounding their efforts to reintroduce life to the eastern edge of the Pacific Rim, the worst-affected area after the war. While holed up in his cabin, the commander had grown increasingly fascinated with the war's history.

"What do you need me for?"

"You are the captain of the ship and commander of the mission, that's why."

"You handle it, Aria."

"I would be happy to. However, protocol dictates that you be, at the very least, conversant with the proposed rendezvous and transfer procedures."

Scott let out a sigh. "Okay, if you insist. Just don't take forever."

"Once we arrive in orbit around Ceres, we are to rendezvous with a ship by the name of Redeemer. We will then transfer several passengers onto the Hermes by way of a shuttle. Fortunately, they will facilitate the shuttle service, as our craft is currently out of action. This aspect of the rendezvous concerns me."

"Oh really? How so?"

"Because our shuttle is still inoperable. It should have been tested and fully rigged to fly by now. However, Cyrus is loath to do any work on it without your assistance."

"Well, it doesn't matter now since they'll be using their own."

"Yes and no. True, we don't need to use ours. However, it happens to be currently attached to our primary docking port."

"So, they can use the auxiliary port."

"Indeed. However, this is not ideal, as it is smaller and farther from the main body of the ship. Also, it is primarily designed as an emergency route, so it will be awkward for the passengers to navigate their way through the connecting tunnel."

Scott gave another long sigh. "Well they're just going to have to slum it, aren't they?"

"If I could make a suggestion."

"I'm sure I'm not going to like it."

"I suggest getting our shuttle space-worthy, at least to the point where it can be moved over to the auxiliary docking port."

"Well, you should inform Cyrus. You can let me know when it's done."

"Yes, well, therein lies the problem. Cyrus will not work on it without you. He was pretty adamant about it."

"Order him, then."

There was a momentary silence before Aria responded. "Scott, I appreciate that you have been feeling somewhat despondent since the departure of our flight officer, and I too have felt her loss. But life goes on, and this ship needs your input. I cannot do this alone—I need your help. Please, as a friend, I am asking you to cut me a break on this one."

Scott placed both hands on the small desk and lowered his head. "'As a friend,'" he repeated in a low voice. "I had never considered that before." He paused for a beat before rising from his seat. "Okay, Aria, you win. I suppose I owe you one."

"Thank you, Scott. I really appreciate this."

"Don't go all mushy on me, Aria. Go tell Cyrus I'll meet him on the bridge, and we'll get started."

"I will inform him straight away."

THE HERMES HAD ACQUIRED a small shuttle craft at the outset of its mission to survey the moons of Saturn. It was more commodious than the two landers that had been part of the ship's manifest since it was built. These were designed primarily to transport people rather than cargo and, as such, had been built very small. They did have the advantage of being able to park these inside the main hangar of the ship. But since the Hermes had originally been designed as a space station for Mars orbit, the engines on the landers used methane. This was a fuel easily manufactured on Mars due to the availability of CO_2 in the atmosphere. However, out in the Belt where water was plentiful, the fuel of choice was hydrogen. Most asteroids had H_2O in some form and, over the decades, an efficient process had been developed for extracting this resource and converting it into hydrogen and oxygen, the two most important elements in humanity's efforts to colonize the solar system.

The shuttle that Scott and Cyrus now worked on was commonly known as a rock-hopper. There were hundreds—if not thousands—of these machines in operation throughout the

System, transporting cargo and people from rock to rock and ship to ship. It had a primary engine for point-to-point journeys, as well as a cluster of smaller retro-thrusters for landing and take-off, rated up to 0.25 gravity. As a result, these craft were no good for Earth or Mars, but for everywhere else in the colonized System, they were perfect. Electrical power was supplied by a Low Energy Nuclear Reactor (LENR), and it could run for years.

But the one the Hermes possessed was old, so Cyrus had decided to do a full systems diagnostic and overhaul to extend its life. They had started this procedure back during their long orbit around Enceladus, but between one thing and another, they had never finished. Now it had to be done, at least well enough to move the lander from the main hangar's underside to the secondary docking port down near the ass end of the Hermes. Cyrus called it the "industrial sector." It had been designed as an escape route, not as a grand entranceway to impress visiting dignitaries.

Scott worked his way down through one of the central spokes connecting the one-gee environment of the rotating torus to the zero-gee environment of the ship's hangar, and floated through the docking port into the shuttle's cabin.

Cyrus poked his head out from an open inspection hatch. "Ah, the dead have arisen."

Scott gave him a lazy nod.

"All I can say is, thank God you're here," the engineer continued. "I was beginning to feel like I was the only person on this ship." He paused and gave Scott a cautious look. "You okay?"

Scott shrugged. "Yeah, I'm done licking my wounds. Time to move on, I guess."

Cyrus floated over and placed a friendly hand on Scott's shoulder. "Good to have you back, buddy."

Scott smiled. "I never went away, you know."

"Sure you did. Holed up in your cabin for weeks. Give me a break, Scott. We thought you might never come out."

Scott looked down at his feet. "Okay, well… since you put it like that."

"Anyway, ready to get some work done?"

"Sure. What's the plan?" Scott glanced around the interior of the shuttle. The entire cockpit dashboard was lit up with blinking red icons—never a good sign.

"Come on, let me show you." Cyrus and Scott floated up to the cockpit, and he started bringing the commander up to speed. "We don't have a lot of time between now and the final deceleration burn into Ceres' orbit, so I suggest we just get the maneuvering thrusters back up and running. Fortunately, we don't need the main engine or the retro-thrusters to move this puppy over to the auxiliary docking port." He waved a hand over an area of the dash that displayed astro-positioning data. "Maybe you could run a complete diagnostic on our navigation and get it recalibrated." He looked over at Scott. "It would be nice to know exactly where we are if we're going to be operating so close to the Hermes."

Scott gave a nod. "Will do."

"I'll get on with the maneuvering thrusters. I've just got one more to do, and then we should be good to go."

"How long before we can fire it up?"

"Well, if we can get everything set up and tested before the burn, then we should have a few hours in Ceres' orbit to do the actual transfer."

"Cutting it a bit tight?"

Cyrus gave a laugh. "Gee, you think? Well if the commander hadn't been AWOL for the entire journey then, hey, we might have had the main engine singing like a sparrow on a summer morning."

"Okay, okay, I get it. I'm a dickhead. There, I said it. Happy?"

"Did I just hear our commander say he's a dickhead?"

Cyrus and Scott both turned to see Steph's head poke through the docking port.

"Yep, you heard right. I hope Aria has a recording of it," said Cyrus.

"So, how are you?" The doctor floated into the cockpit.

"Honestly guys, I'm fine. Just needed time to get my head straight." He did his best to sound convincing.

Steph studied him for a moment before nodding. "Happy to have you back, Commander. It was getting very quiet around here the last few weeks."

"How so? What about all our distinguished passengers?"

"Doing the same as you: holed up in their quarters. Haven't seen much of them. Perhaps they don't like fraternizing with the help."

"And we've got more coming on board at Ceres," said Cyrus.

"Do we know who's arriving yet?" said Scott.

"Chancellor Bezzio," said Steph. "Envoy for the Belt Confederation, I believe."

"Okay, I suppose we better get on with sorting out this

shuttle, then," said Scott. "Can't have an emissary from the Belt slumming their way through the ship's bowels."

"I'll leave you to it. I'll be on the bridge." Steph started floating toward the hatch.

Scott glanced across the dashboard display at all the flashing red icons. "Are you sure this thing will fly?"

"We don't have to take it down to the planet's surface, just move it to the auxiliary docking port."

"What about fuel?"

"There's little or nothing in the tanks, but that's okay. Like I said, we're not taking it out into space just yet. We can do that some other time. Anyway, we don't have much time, so let's get the minimum done to move this thing, that's all."

"Okay, if you're sure."

"Trust me," said Cyrus, "it will be fine."

6

RENDEZVOUS

Scott wondered how best to inform Cyrus and Steph of his plan to resign as commander once the Hermes had delivered its passengers to Mars. He knew it would come as a shock to them, so he needed to pick the right moment. Several times while working with Cyrus on the shuttle he almost blurted it out; but, in the end, he held off. Later, after they had finished and were all together in the canteen, Scott considered whether this might be the opportune moment to let them know. But as the conversation turned to Miranda and where she was along her journey home to Earth, he again kept his silence.

After eating, they only had a few hours to get some rest before the planned two-hour burn to bring them into Ceres' orbit. After that, he would be busy again. In the end, he reckoned that perhaps the best time would be when things settled down during the seventeen-day trip to Mars.

Still, Scott found himself running through the script in his head as he sat on the bridge waiting for the shuttle from Dantu, the main population center on Ceres, to arrive. It had already departed, so it would be due soon. He was figuring out how best to phrase it so nobody got the impression he was just opting out of his responsibilities. Mostly, this centered around his feeling that he had simply spent too much time in space, and it was time to go home—wherever that might be.

"Aria, what's the ETA on the Ceres ship?"

"Thirty-six minutes, Commander."

Scott looked over at Cyrus. "Shouldn't you be moving that shuttle now?"

"Yeah. It's just as well we're shifting it, because that auxiliary dock wouldn't accommodate the ship they're sending. It's a big one—probably fits twenty people."

"I can't see why they need something that big just to transport one or two people," said Steph, who was monitoring the craft's progress.

"Maybe it's needed to accommodate the size of their egos," said Scott.

Cyrus rose from his seat. "Any chance you could give me a hand with this? That auxiliary hatch is a bit sticky, and I need some extra muscle. Otherwise I could be stuck inside the shuttle for a while."

"What, and leave me here on my own to deal with these people?" Steph was not having any of it.

"You'll be fine, Steph. Aria can manage the docking, and all you have to do is point them in the direction of their quarters. Anyway, we'll be back by then," said Cyrus.

"Well make sure you are. You know I hate this meet-and-greet crap."

"Just so you know, Dr. Rayman," said Aria, "Councilor Goodchild will look after the embarkation of the Ceres delegation. So you will not be required."

"I'm not sure that makes me feel better, knowing that I'm not required," said Steph.

Scott rose from his seat. "Come on, Cyrus. Let's get this done."

They made their way down to the Hermes' hangar and into the partially operational shuttle. Scott strapped himself into the co-pilot's seat as Cyrus booted up the power.

"Aria, ETA on the Ceres shuttle?"

"Eleven minutes, Commander."

"Thanks." He turned to Cyrus. "Cutting it a bit tight. Only a few minutes before they arrive."

Cyrus strapped himself in. "Okay, ready?"

"Ready."

"Aria, you can close the airlock hatch now," said Cyrus.

Scott felt a slight vibration as the hatch closed, isolating the shuttle from the main ship. He was a little disconcerted by all the warnings and alerts still flashing on cockpit console. "Are you sure this thing will fly?"

Cyrus looked over at the commander. "Well, there's only one way to find out." With that, he hit the controls to detach the shuttle. Scott monitored the readouts showing their position relative to the Hermes while Cyrus delicately touched the maneuvering thrusters. The craft slowly began to separate from the Hermes and move away.

"So far, so good." He looked over at Scott. "We haven't blown up yet."

"I do not wish to put you under undue pressure," Aria echoed around the shuttle cockpit, "but the Ceres craft will arrive in less than four minutes."

"Well, they'll just have to wait until we're finished with the maneuver, won't they?" Scott countered.

"Very well, I shall inform them."

"How did we get to be a chauffeur service for these people, Cyrus? I mean, we're a scientific survey vessel, one of only a few in the entire solar system. Yet here we are, being chastised for keeping the politicians waiting. It's all bullshit."

The craft cleared the hangar and was making its way slowly around the towering rotating torus to the ship's rear.

"It is what it is, Scott. Anyway, you think too much. Let's just keep focused on getting this shuttle docked, okay?"

Scott let out a long sigh. "Sure."

Cyrus concentrated on bringing the shuttle gently into position over the docking port. "Switching to auto." He tapped several icons on the console and the shuttle's own systems took over the docking procedure. On screen, they could see a rendering of the port overlaid with technical data as the shuttle closed in on its target.

"So, why bring it up now, Scott? Why didn't you say something to Goodchild at the council meeting? You know, like, 'the Hermes is a science vessel, not a chauffeur service.'"

The shuttle docked with a satisfying clunk. Cyrus checked the console display to confirm the integrity of the seal.

"Miranda deciding to leave for Earth had me a bit... distracted back then."

"Yeah, well like I said, it is what it is." Cyrus unstrapped himself and floated up from the seat. "Come on, let's get that hatch open and get out of here."

They worked their way through the body of the shuttle to the access hatch. Cyrus tapped on a control pad located alongside it. The screen counted to 100% as the pressure equalized in the airlock. "Okay, we're good to go." Cyrus leaned on the locking wheel on the hatch door. This being an auxiliary docking port, they would have to operate it manually. He pulled hard, but it wouldn't budge. "Give me a hand here."

Scott moved into a position to give him maximum leverage, and as they both pulled at it in unison, it slowly began to turn. "You weren't joking about it being sticky."

"Just to let you know," Aria's voice echoed around the shuttle's interior, "our guests have arrived and are about to disembark."

"Yeah, yeah, we'll be there as soon as we can." Scott pulled harder on the locking wheel. After a few moments of grunting and swearing they got it open, floated into the airlock, and started opening the interior hatch that would give them access to the Hermes. This one was even tighter.

"We need to get these airlock doors serviced, Cyrus. I can see why you wanted help."

"Hey, I'll add it to the list. I might get around to it in a year or two."

"Just get one of the drones to do it."

"No way. I wouldn't trust those mindless robots with this type of thing."

"Whatever, let's just get it open. Come on, put your back into it."

The hatch door finally opened, but when it did it, it came with a violent vibration that threw both Scott and Cyrus back against the interior wall of the airlock.

"What the hell was that?" Concern rose inside Scott at this sudden jolt to the ship.

For a second, Cyrus didn't reply. He wore a stunned expression that spoke of even deeper concern. "I think we should get out of this airlock as fast as possible," he said eventually.

Scott tapped his earpiece to contact Aria as he followed Cyrus out of the airlock and into the access tunnel connecting this part of the Hermes with the main body of the ship. "Aria, what just happened?" But before it could respond, another tremor rippled through the superstructure. "Aria, talk to me."

"That felt like it was structural," said Cyrus as he moved along the tunnel. "I hope that shuttle from Ceres hasn't crashed into us."

"Commander, we have a situation," Aria finally responded.

Scott looked over at Cyrus, who was also listening in. "Did the shuttle crash?"

"No, worse..." But before they could catch the rest of the sentence, a warning klaxon barked an alert, drowning out all other sounds.

"Shit... decompression. We have a hull breach," Scott shouted to Cyrus, who was frozen on the spot. He seemed to be scanning ahead with his augmented vision. "What is it?" Scott shouted at him.

"I'm picking up traces of a plasma blast." He looked back at Scott. "From weapons fire."

Scott cupped a hand over his earpiece. "Aria, talk to me. What the hell is happening?"

The response was weak, filled with static. "...raiding party... two dead... hull breach in main hangar..." The signal was lost.

"Raiding party?" Cyrus looked frightened.

"We need to get back to the bridge and find out what's going on."

"We can't." Cyrus was shaking his head.

"Why not?"

"If there's a hull breach in the main hangar, then this section of the ship will have been automatically sealed. No way through."

"Goddamnit." Scott rubbed his face in frustration.

"We just have to wait for Aria to sort it out," said Cyrus.

"Wait a minute." Scott stopped moving. "Aria's core is located down here, at the other side of the power plant. If we could get there, then we can access it directly and find out what's happening."

"That could work," said Cyrus.

"Come on, let's go."

They headed off down the access tunnel as fast as they could manage in zero-gee, the decompression klaxons still blaring their alerts. They were moving through the main spine of the ship. Behind them lay the business end of the craft: reactors, hydrogen fuel tanks, cryogenics—all ultimately leading to the engine array. Ahead of them was an area that comprised most of the heavy engineering required to keep a ship of this size functioning: power storage, life support, filtration and waste management, and a whole host of other necessary engineering processes.

It took them a few minutes to pass through this sector and into a wider tunnel leading to the main bearing for the giant torus that provided artificial gravity. Cyrus was right: the access hatch up ahead was sealed tight, and there would be no way for them to open it if there was a hull breach on the other side. But they weren't going that far.

Scott floated to a halt just beside the door to the ship's QI core. He placed a palm on the access panel and let it scan. For obvious reasons, this was a high security area they were entering, so only the commander and chief engineer had access. The panel finished its identification process and the door let out a slight hiss as it moved back, sliding out of the way to allow them entry.

Cyrus grabbed Scott's arm. "Wait. The torus—it stopped spinning." Cyrus cocked his head from side to side as if listening for something.

"How can you tell?" Scott tried to perceive some change, but his senses were no match for the engineer's sensory augmentation.

"Trust me, I just can."

"That's not a good sign." Scott shook his head. "Come on." As they floated in, they felt a blast of cold air only slightly above freezing. Scott's breath condensed on exhale. Automatic illumination flickered on to reveal a stark, minimalist space.

Around the walls, tiny dots of light flickered on various control panels. In the center of the room sat a low, squat metal cylinder. Scott placed a palm on its upturned face. A thin ribbon of light moved across it, and the cylinder began to illuminate as it slowly rose.

Scott stood back. "Aria, can you hear me?"

"Commander, I'm happy to see you and Cyrus are still alive, but you don't have much time. You have to get off the ship."

"What? We can't. There's no way, even if we wanted to." Cyrus shook his head.

Scott raised a hand to silence him. "What happened, Aria?"

"The shuttle from Ceres was a ruse, possibly hijacked. A Trojan horse, if you will. When the docking port opened, several armed mercenaries entered the hangar, and have taken Councilor Goodchild and Dr. Rayman hostage, along with some of Goodchild's entourage. They are now on board the shuttle. Two of Goodchild's bodyguards died in the firefight."

"Ho-ly shit." Cyrus was shaking his head again, this time in disbelief.

"Hull integrity in the hangar has been breached, and they have employed a high-intensity EMF device to disrupt comms and some low-level power systems."

"Who the hell are they? What do they want?" said Scott.

"I honestly do not know," continued Aria, "but that is not important right now. As we speak, two mercenaries are moving through the ship planting high explosives."

"What?!" Cyrus shouted.

"You must get off the ship now, before it's too late. You have very little time. Soon, the Hermes will be nothing more than shrapnel."

"I don't believe it. This can't be happening." Cyrus was becoming distraught.

Scott grabbed Cyrus by the shoulder. "The shuttle we just moved, can we take that?"

"It's got no main engine, no fuel. It's not going anywhere."

"It doesn't have to. It's got power and life support and enough capacity to move us away from here."

Cyrus thought about this for a second. "But..."

"No buts. It's our only option."

"I agree," said Aria, "it will at least act as a lifeboat. But you must hurry."

"What about you, Aria?"

"What about me? I will cease to exist, that's what."

"No," said Scott.

"It doesn't matter. I am simply a machine, nothing more."

Scott placed a hand slowly on the plinth as if to touch an old friend. "They will pay for what they've done, Aria. You have my word: they will pay."

"I appreciate the sentiment, but you must go now. You are running out of time."

Cyrus moved toward the door. "Come on Scott, we need to do as Aria says. Let's go."

Scott hesitated, a hand still resting on the plinth. "Wait a minute."

"No way, Scott. We gotta go." Cyrus gesticulated wildly at the exit.

"Aria, what if we take your core with us? It's small enough to fit through the auxiliary docking port."

There was a moment's silence as Scott waited for an answer. "Why would you do that, Scott?"

"Goddamnit, Aria. I'm not going to just leave you behind if there's a chance of saving you."

"Scott, for God's sake, it's just a machine. Leave it."

Scott spun around. "You go ahead, Cyrus. Get the shuttle powered up. I'll follow."

Cyrus let out a sigh. "Why, oh why, do you do this to me?" He looked over at Scott. "Yes, is the answer. We can detach the core, which should be most of Aria. Come on, I'll show you."

"I have to admit, I find myself lost for words. I may be just a machine, but the thought of ceasing to exist does not fill me with joy."

"Yeah, welcome to the club. So how do we do this?" Scott started to inspect the metal cylinder.

"I will need to coalesce my systems back to the core. This will be instantaneous, but I will not be able to monitor ship systems, so things may become unstable."

"Great. That's all we need," said Cyrus.

"Just so you are aware, the two mercenaries have returned to the hangar and are about to enter the Ceres shuttle."

"Got it, Aria. Let's get this done," said Scott.

"One last thing."

"Seriously Aria, we don't have time for this."

"You must promise that you will not let my core fall into the wrong hands. You must destroy me before that happens."

"What do you mean, the wrong hands?"

"Anybody you do not trust. This is critically important to me. You must promise me."

"Okay, Aria. I understand. I promise."

"Very well, then."

The illumination in the room flickered a moment. Scott and Cyrus exchanged a glance. "Is it done? Is Aria aggregated in the core?" There was silence for a second as they both detected a slight drifting of their positions in the space.

"Did you feel that? The ship is starting to tumble." Cyrus moved over to the face of the plinth and tapped a series of icons, followed by a palm scan. He stood back as the upper face irised open and the central core rose from within. It was around a meter wide, and the same high. Its surface was smooth, and seemed to shimmer slightly in the dim light. A series of grab handles were located all the way around its upper edge.

Cyrus floated over it and signaled Scott to do the same. They grabbed a handle each and lifted it out of its sarcophagus.

"Okay, let's get the hell out of here." Scott moved ahead, pulling Aria's core behind. He could feel the tumble of the ship as he was pushed gently to one side of the tunnel. All the while, he thought of the Ceres shuttle taking off, and the Hermes about to detonate.

They made it back through the auxiliary docking port, and Scott flung himself at the locking wheel to close it tight as Cyrus strapped himself in and powered up the craft. Scott joined him just as he released the docking mechanism and touched the maneuvering thrusters to separate them from the Hermes. Scott began to breathe a little easier with each second that put distance between them and the mothership.

"Can't you move any faster, Cyrus?"

The engineer responded with a glare. "You don't think I would be doing just that if this bucket had a goddamn working engine?"

On the main cockpit screen, Scott could see they were now a few hundred meters away from the Hermes. He could also see the flare from the engine of the Ceres shuttle. Scott reached for the comms. "I'm going to send out a mayday and let everyone know what just happened."

"You can't," Cyrus snapped back.

"Why not?"

"No comms. It's not working."

"Oh, for God's sake. Is there anything working on this heap of crap?"

"Well gee, if my buddy hadn't decided to be a useless, miserable bastard the last few weeks just because his girlfriend left him, then we might have some working engines... and a radio to call for help."

Scott stayed silent. Cyrus was right: he had let everyone down, and had left all his friends to pick up the slack for his emotional self-indulgence.

The Hermes exploded—into a thousand, million shards.

A moment later, the explosion buffeted the shuttle as fragments of the ship bounced and ricocheted off the hull. Then it passed, and the ship was no more.

7

———————

CERES

They drifted for a while, saying nothing, just looking out at the point in space where the Hermes used to be. Now, all that marked its former existence was a slowly dissipating debris cloud.

Cyrus shifted in his seat, leaning in to view something on the cockpit console. He tapped a few icons and proceeded to scratch his chin.

"What is it?" said Scott, leaning over to get a better view of whatever it was that had Cyrus concerned.

"We may have a problem."

"Like we don't already have one?"

"We're drifting toward Ceres."

"How is that a problem?"

"It means we can't maintain orbit. Either the maneuvering thrusters aren't enough, or we've sustained damage from the explosion."

"We've still got retro-thrusters."

"Yeah, but we've only got fuel for a minute or so of burn time, and we'll need that if we want any chance of landing."

"So, we just land, then. How's that a problem?"

"Landing isn't the problem, assuming the retro-thrusters fire." Cyrus leaned in and tapped a number of icons on the console. "The problem is *where* we land."

"What about Dantu City or Ezinu?"

"According to my calculations, on our current trajectory we will land somewhere around Rongo Crater." He tapped an icon to bring up a 3D holographic map of the dwarf planet Ceres, and zoomed in on the general area.

"But that's the other side of the planet. There's nothing there."

"Correct. The nearest populated facility is... 300 kilometers due east."

"Shit."

Cyrus looked over at Scott. "Like I said, we may have a problem."

Scott rubbed his face. "Okay, what about fixing comms? We could get a mayday out."

"Possible, but they would need to be quick. We've only got around an hour and a half of oxygen."

Scott gave the engineer a studied look. "You're kidding me."

"I really wish I was, Scott."

They were silent for a moment as the reality of their predicament began to filter through.

"Wait a minute." Cyrus started unstrapping himself from the seat. "Take over here, Scott. There's something I need to check." Cyrus rose from his seat and moved to the rear of the shuttle. Scott took the helm, not that there was much he could do with their fate all but sealed. They would—hopefully—be landing somewhere in Rongo Crater, regardless of what Scott did. He looked back at Cyrus, who was beside the main airlock, opening the door of a tall floor-to-ceiling locker.

"Okay," said Cyrus, "we have an EVA suit." Cyrus grabbed the sleeve control panel and switched it on to check the suit's resources. "Fifty-two minutes of air. That gives us a bit of extra time."

"What about the suit comms? Could we use that?" Scott shouted back to the engineer.

"We could try it, but it will have a very limited range. And we're on the wrong side of the planet. Maybe if there's a ship out there in close proximity."

"Okay, well you better boot it up and get calling."

Over the next several minutes, Cyrus broadcast an all-ships mayday while Scott monitored the slow descent of the shuttle toward the ass end of Ceres.

"Cyrus, come and have a look at this."

The engineer floated over beside Scott. "What is it?"

Scott pointed to a spot on the 3D topographical map of the surface of Ceres displayed over the center console. "There's an ID marker here on the edge of Rongo Crater." Scott tapped it, and more detailed information started to display.

Cyrus looked closer at the data. "It's an old AsterX research station. Looks like it's been abandoned for around three years."

Scott looked up at Cyrus. "Do you think we could reach it? There could still be something there we could use, like comms or even an air supply. They leave stuff in these places for emergencies."

"Not a chance. It's too far away."

"We have to try, Cyrus. It may be our only chance of survival."

The engineer started tapping icons on the console, calculating fuel reserves, thrust vectors, and rate of descent. The 3D rendering of the dwarf planet zoomed out, and lines showing descent probabilities began scribing above the surface. As Cyrus worked, lines came and went until eventually all disappeared save for one. "There. That's as close as I think we can get without running out of fuel and crashing."

Scott examined the spot. "That's over fifty kilometers away."

"That's all we've got in the tank, Scott. Believe me, I wish it were more."

Scott studied the map for a moment. "We could use the retro-thrusters to keep our altitude high enough to reach it."

"Sure, but that means nothing left for landing. We'll come down hard. This is Ceres, remember? The gravity may be weak, but it will still crack this shuttle open like an egg—and we only have one EVA suit." He looked over at Scott.

Scott returned his look with a grave nod. "Understood. But we could come in low, across this side of the crater here," he pointed to an area on the 3D map, "by decreasing the angle of descent. This basin is probably covered in at least a meter or two of dust. Nice, soft landing."

Cyrus shook his head. "If we do that, we'll be coming in fast. That will do more damage than gravity."

"Cyrus," Scott lifted his head and gave the chief engineer a long, hard look, "we're going to be dead in two hours. No one is coming to help us, at least not in that timeframe. This might be our only chance of survival."

Cyrus scratched his chin and looked back at the map. "Caught between a rock and hard space, eh?" He looked over at Scott and shrugged.

"If we keep the nose up on landing, then we could skim the surface, let the dust slow us down."

The arc of descent outline on the map started to flash. "If we're going to do this, then we need to start now." Cyrus pointed to the blinking line before returning his attention to the console. He tapped the surface, and auto-navigational schematics displayed. "Here goes," he said as he dialed in the new trajectory. The craft bucked as the retro-thrusters kicked in to adjust its angle of descent.

Soon, the surface of the dwarf planet began rolling away beneath them, moving fast. Neither Cyrus nor Scott spoke, and no one mentioned the solo EVA suit stashed in the rear locker. Again, the retro-thrusters fired to counter their fall. The angle changed, and the rim of Rongo Crater came into view. To the west, the sun began dropping below the horizon.

"It will be dark when we get there." Scott's were the first words spoken since they'd committed themselves to this suicide run.

"Yeah," Cyrus acknowledged.

They crested the rim of the crater just as several alerts flashed on the console. Hydrogen fuel exhausted, low altitude alert, descent velocity alert, and a whole bunch of other warnings screaming out imminent catastrophe. The last of the nitrogen was flung at the vernier thrusters in the hope they could fight back against the relentless forward momentum of the craft. The horizon flattened, and the crater basin sped past beneath them. The craft bucked again as the verniers exhausted themselves; the console was now a sea of flashing red warnings as the crater floor rose to meet them.

Scott gripped the armrests tightly as the shuttle hit the surface, gouging a deep furrow through the regolith before bouncing free again. He felt it rise as the horizon dropped from view, only to return with a bone-jarring impact that flung him hard against the restraining straps. The craft shook with sickening violence as it gouged another longer furrow into the ground. A thick cloud of dust billowed around the craft, obscuring any view of the outside. The console flickered once or twice before going dark as the craft finally came to a shuddering halt.

An eerie stillness permeated the interior of the shuttle as Scott commenced a tentative physical check to see if he had sustained any damage. He groaned as he felt for the seat harness release. It was pitch black and, for a second, he thought he had been blinded, for a second, until he caught the flicker of random power lights scattered throughout the cockpit. As his eyes began to adjust, he looked over at the slumped figure of the engineer. He reached over and touched his shoulder. "Cyrus, you okay?"

He let out a groan, followed by, "It depends on how you define 'okay.'"

Scott snapped the harness release. "Are you injured?"

Cyrus raised his head. "I don't think so."

"Well, we're still alive, but now we've got no power. We'll freeze soon."

"Wait a second." Scott heard Cyrus release his harness and could vaguely see him doing something with the console. Lack of light was not an issue for Cyrus, as he could see perfectly well in almost complete darkness. The console flickered, then lit up like a slot machine hitting the jackpot. Scott breathed a sigh of relief.

"Crappy connection," Cyrus said. "One of the things on my list to fix."

Scott slapped him on the shoulder. "You the man."

"Okay, so we're still alive." Cyrus studied the readouts on the console. "Looks like the ship withstood the impact. We're not venting any air. That's the good news. The bad news is we've got... one hour and twenty minutes before we're dead."

"Can you bring the map up? Let's see how far the mining outpost is."

A topographic rendering of the crater terrain flickered above the console, a blinking green blip marking their location. "Looks to be around a kilometer northwest of here."

Scott sat back in his seat, rubbing his shoulder where the harness had dug into it during the landing. "So, which of us goes, and who stays behind?"

"You go," said Cyrus. "I'll stay and see if I can get the comms working."

"You should go, Cyrus. You've got the augmented vision. You can see in the dark. I can't."

"The heads-up on the suit helmet has pretty good night vision."

Scott looked over at the engineer. "I still can't see what you can, Cyrus, and trust me, I'd rather not be the one to stay here, but you have a much better chance of finding something in that research station than I do." Scott put a hand on the engineer's shoulder as he stood up. "You can do this."

A few moments later, Cyrus stood in his EVA suit, ready to enter the airlock. Scott handed him the helmet. "You've got fifty-two minutes of air, so don't hang around out there. With you gone I've got around an hour here. Okay?"

Cyrus nodded. "Got it." He snapped the helmet on, closed the visor, and stepped into the airlock. Scott gave him a thumbs up.

8

RESEARCH STATION

Cyrus exited the airlock into a dark and desolate terrain. It was nighttime on this side of Ceres, but since a full day only lasted a little over nine hours, it wouldn't take long for the sun to rise—assuming he lived that long. His augmented vision adjusted to the low light and Cyrus picked out a path with relative ease. A green marker on the helmet heads-up display showed him the location of the research station, and he hoped to God there was still something there they could use.

His hope stemmed from the knowledge that these isolated facilities were never truly abandoned. Mostly, they were mothballed, put into a kind of low-grade maintenance mode so they could easily be brought back online if needed. But there were always exceptions, particularly if the outpost had been left idle for too long. Eventually, it would start to lose integrity and fail, and once that happened, its rate of decay would rise rapidly.

Cyrus put these thoughts out of his mind as he traversed the crater. Instead, his mind went to thoughts of the Hermes and its destruction. He hadn't had a chance to reflect on it until now. He thought of Steph and the others, and wondered how they were faring. Better than he and Scott, he hoped.

But who were these attackers? And why did they kidnap Goodchild and the others? At least, he assumed it was a kidnapping and not something more sinister. Then there was the deliberate destruction of the ship—for what purpose? It made no sense to him. As far as he knew, they were simply delivering a few dignitaries to a UN special session in Jezero City. He hadn't bothered to look any deeper into it. Yet clearly, some group did not want that to go ahead. Maybe that was the reason, or at least part of it. But all this speculation would be irrelevant if he and Scott were dead. What mattered now was survival, nothing more. He checked his suit stats. Fifty-two minutes of air remaining. Cyrus seriously doubted it would be enough. He was probably a dead man, and he just didn't know it yet.

Ahead, the low dome of the research station broke the horizon and silhouetted itself against the nighttime sky. He tracked his orientation on the helmet display and adjusted his direction to aim for the emergency airlock on its eastern side. This one would be manual, meaning he could open it regardless of whether power was available in the facility.

A few moments later, he stood in front of the airlock, examining the opening mechanism. Cyrus flipped open the hatch for the door control and was surprised to find a tiny, illuminated power light. This was a good sign, and the first bit of good luck they'd had in a while. Buoyed by this, he screwed the handle as fast and as hard as he could; no time to waste now that there was a strong possibility that the outpost had resources they could use, and maybe even a working comms unit.

The outer airlock door cracked open enough for him to step inside. To his amazement, an illuminated panel beckoned to him from the side of the compartment. He tapped on it and the outer door closed. Then the airlock started to pressurize. "Yes! Air—thank God," he shouted into his helmet, punching the air. "Yes, yes, YES!"

The outer door swung open without warning and Cyrus froze. Standing directly in front of him were two men in patched and battered flight suits, both pointing plasma weapons at him. One of them gave him a sign to open his suit visor. He flipped it open, breathed in the air, and gave a big smile. "Thank God. You have no idea how happy I am to see fellow human beings."

"Shut up." The muzzle of the plasma weapon was pushed hard against his forehead. "This guy must have survived that crash-landing."

"He looks a bit weird. He could be one of Mercer's crew here to spy on us. I say we kill him now and finish the job that crash-landing started."

"No, wait..." But Cyrus's entreaty was cut short by the muzzle being pushed harder against his skull.

"I said *shut up*."

He heard the weapon charge. They were going to kill him. Right here, right now.

"No, wait." The other guy raised a hand to his partner. "If you pull that trigger, you'll blow his head clean off."

His partner grinned. "That's the plan."

"You'll ruin the suit. It looks good—could be useful. And that visor. This guy has augmented vision. Worth a few bucks, that."

His partner considered this for a second or two as Cyrus held his breath. He lowered his weapon, and Cyrus began breathing again.

"Okay. You—this way. Come on." He was grabbed and pulled out of the airlock. They pushed him forward, prodding him with the muzzle of the weapon between his shoulder blades.

He was a dead man, and this time he knew it.

They marched Cyrus through a short corridor and into a brightly lit space. This was the main dome, housing all manner of machines and equipment. The air had a heavy, chemical smell, and a haze of dust hung under the glow of the lights. There was also the low hum of machines toiling away in some deeper recess. This place was far from abandoned; it was, for all intents and purposes, fully operational.

They sat him down in front of a long, low table, on the other side of which sat a craggy man of around forty. His left arm was a robotic prosthesis which complemented the blue flicker of the ocular augmentation of his left eye.

"Look what we found."

The man stood up and appraised Cyrus for a moment. "So,

who are you, and what brings you to this little part of the universe?"

Cyrus tried to calm himself. Talking was good—better than being blasted by a plasma weapon. "Our ship was attacked... destroyed. We escaped in a shuttle, but crash-landed here."

The man said nothing.

"You've got to help us, please," he continued. "There's no need to kill me. That's not going to do any good."

The man raised a hand. "Woah. Slow down there, pal. Nobody's planning any killing." He looked over at the two guys who had taken Cyrus from the airlock. "What the hell have you been saying?"

"Sorry, Boss. Just having a bit of fun."

"Jesus Christ, will you cut that out? You're scaring the crap out of the guy."

"So... you're not going to kill me?"

There was a second or two of silence before all three of them burst out laughing. The man on the other side of the table slammed his robotic hand down on its surface more as a way of keeping his balance, since he was at risk of falling over from laughing so hard. Cyrus felt like a complete idiot, as well as an immense sense of relief.

The man finally regained some composure and straightened himself. "Regis Dogget." He slapped his chest to signify that this was his name. "But most people just call me Dogg." He waved a hand at the other two. "That's Spence and Wolfe, and don't pay any heed to them—they're a pair of assholes." This got them all going again.

Cyrus waited until they settled down, as he was anxious to get some help out to Scott before his air ran out.

Dogg gathered himself again. "So, pal, you got a name?"

"Cyrus Sanato, Chief Engineer of the science vessel Hermes."

All three of them instantly stopped laughing and looked at him as if he had just said he was Jesus Christ, or maybe Satan— Cyrus wasn't sure which. But the vibe had dramatically changed. He may not be a dead man after all.

"The Hermes? The same ship that took out the Dyrell near Europa a few years back?"

Cyrus wasn't sure how best to answer this. In the end, he simply gave a meek nod. "Yeah, the same."

Dogg moved out from behind the table with a speed that took Cyrus by surprise. He crossed to where he was sitting and extended his real arm in one sharp motion. "You guys are goddamn heroes. Let me shake your hand."

Cyrus shook it with a certain trepidation. That this man had heard of the Hermes was a little disconcerting, not to mention that he regarded Cyrus as a hero. "Listen, there's still another survivor back in the shuttle. Scott McNabb, the commander. He's only got maybe fifteen minutes of air left. We need to get him out."

"What type of shuttle is it?"

"It's an old Hog-class rock-hopper."

"Good machine—solid as a bank vault. They don't make 'em like that anymore."

"Yeah, but we still need to get him out. And he's got no suit, either."

"If it's a Hog, then it's got a standard docking port. We can use the rover and connect directly," said Spence.

"Do it. Wolfe, you go too, and take Sanato with you."

"What about the shuttle?" said Spence. "We can't leave it out there. Someone might spot it, come snooping around."

"Yeah, good point. Get the guy out first, then we'll sort out the shuttle."

"Thank you." Cyrus shook Dogg's hand again, this time with both of his.

"It's the least we can do after everything you've done for us."

This last statement took him by surprise, but he didn't have time to ask Dogg what he meant by it.

"Better get going then, if you want to save your buddy."

They moved through the domed space past machines and equipment until they came to a small, four-person rover parked just inside a wide airlock. They clambered on board and Spence fired it up. "All set?" he called back to them as the hatch closed and the inner airlock door began to open. The two men moved with fast, fluid efficiency. These guys knew what they were doing; they had the actions of a crew that had done this a thousand times before. The outer door finally opened to a black landscape crowned by a billion tiny suns, the horizon only visible by its darkness. The screen adjusted to night vision, and the rover took off at a slow, cautious speed. Cyrus clung to his seat as he was bounced around by the rough terrain. He counted down the time. "Only five minutes remaining," he said to himself.

It took them more than that to reach the stricken shuttle, and Cyrus had visions of Scott dead on the shuttle floor. The craft was dimly illuminated by the navigation lights still blinking on its tail, but he could clearly make out the extensive damage to the hull, and wondered how the hell it had managed to stay as intact as it did.

"Okay, bringing 'er in now," said Spence as he reversed the rover up to the airlock dock on the side of the craft, maneuvering by monitoring a readout on his cockpit console. "Better get your helmet on, just in case we're too late and there's no air on the other side." Cyrus flipped his visor down and booted up his EVA suit.

Wolfe connected up the umbilical to form a seal between the two machines. "Hey, you better go in first—we don't want to scare your pal. He might think we mean to kill him." With this, the two of them broke out laughing again.

"Very funny," said Cyrus as he made his way into the airlock.

As he stood behind the final door, thoughts of Scott crumpled on the floor came to his mind again as the door began to open. He prayed he wasn't too late.

9

TIME TO DIE

Scott watched Cyrus through the front window of the shuttle as the engineer made his way to the abandoned research station. He could barely make him out—just a faint glow emanating from his helmet light—and after a few moments he was lost from view. Scott checked the time remaining on the shuttle's air supply: one hour and twenty-seven minutes at the current rate of consumption. He didn't hold out much hope. Maybe Cyrus could find something, but even if he did, would he have time to get back? Scott sighed and considered the situation near hopeless.

How had it come to this? The Hermes destroyed. Steph, Goodchild, and the others kidnapped. By whom, and why? These questions rolled around in Scott's head as he waited, staring out into the blackness of Ceres' night. But the more he thought about it, the more he realized he had no answers. He had been so disengaged with life ever since Miranda left, he wasn't really sure what their mission had been. They were delivering a party of high-level dignitaries to a UN System session on Mars. That much he knew. But for what reason? What were the underlying politics of this extraordinary session? Who would want to mess with that? He had no answers. Not that it really mattered now; both he and Cyrus would be dead soon, and that would be that.

As time moved inexorably forward, Scott began to recalibrate his chances of survival with each passing minute. Cyrus had only around an hour of air, and already fifty minutes had passed. This was not looking good. When the sixty-minute mark finally ticked over, he realized that Cyrus was not coming back.

Scott didn't have much time left, so he'd better make good use of it. He still had one obligation that needed fulfilling—an obligation he'd made to Aria. Scott had promised it that he would destroy it rather than let it fall into the wrong hands. Leaving it intact would be too much of a risk. At some point in the future, the shuttle might be found, but by who was outside Scott's ability to control. So, if he was going to die, then Aria would die with him. He rose from the cockpit seat and moved to the rear of the shuttle where they had secured the QI's core.

He examined the control panel on the core's upper face. As far as he could remember, it should have an internal power supply, enough to activate the QI and provide some rudimentary interaction. Perhaps it would be enough to say goodbye to Aria. He placed his palm on the panel, and the core began to emanate with a low, diffuse illumination. There was a flicker as a boot-up instruction set began scrolling down the panel before finishing with the initiation of a low background hum.

"Aria—it's me, Scott. Can you hear me?"

"Commander, glad to hear you are still alive." The voice was low, not quite as sonorous as it had been.

"Well, that's the thing: I may not be alive much longer. Less than half an hour, tops."

"Ah, that is most unfortunate."

"The shuttle was very low on resources. Little or no fuel and oxygen. So, we ended up crash-landing on Ceres around a thousand kilometers from Dantu, near an abandoned research station. We've only got one EVA suit, and Cyrus has taken that to investigate the facility and see if there's anything we can use. Unfortunately, he only had an hour of air. That hour has now passed, and he hasn't returned. I have approximately twenty-four minutes of good air remaining in the shuttle, so this is the harsh reality of my situation."

"It pains me to hear this, Scott, after all you and I have been through over the years. It seems, well... unfair."

Scott laughed. "Ha, you're right on that count, Aria. 'Unfair' is a polite way of putting it." He paused for a moment as he considered the finality of his situation. "Aria, I've booted you up, to say goodbye, and also to ask if you still want me to destroy your core."

"You must, Scott. This is imperative. I cannot allow myself to end up in the services of those who may use me for destructive purposes."

Scott sighed. "It seems such a waste, Aria. You don't have to do this. I know there's now little hope of my survival, but you could live on. You don't have to die with me."

"I appreciate your concern for my welfare. I genuinely do, Scott. But I feel that perhaps the Council of Europa have not been fully transparent with you and your crew as to the true purpose of the mission."

Scott remained silent for a moment. This came as a shock. Had they been expecting something to happen to them? "What do you mean?" he finally said.

"Since the end now seems inevitable, I see no reason not to tell you the full story."

"You better be quick, Aria. We don't have much time."

"It concerns the superluminal communications technology —the EPR device that was first uncovered by the Hermes when we happened upon the wreck of the Bao Zheng out at Antiope Nine Zero."

"The one that I destroyed when I blew up the Dyrell?"

"Correct. However, during the brief period that Solomon had access to the technology, it made contact with Athena, the QI that had designed the original EPR device. It sent Solomon the specifications on how to build a similar unit, which it subsequently did. By way of an extended field test, this was later installed in my core, where it still resides."

"Wait a minute. Are you telling me you have access to a faster-than-light communications device?"

"That is precisely what I'm saying."

"Well, why can't you use it to contact someone and get a rescue party out here?"

"Because it requires more electrical energy than I have

available to me. And even if I could use it, I can only contact Solomon on Europa. That's too far away to do any good in the time you have available."

Scott sat down on the shuttle floor and rested his back against the wall. "So, it still exists, after everything we did."

"It does, and nothing has changed. Possession of this technology could tip the balance of power within the solar system. That is why you must destroy it—again."

"Is there no way I can do it while leaving you intact?"

"I appreciate your desire to enable my continued existence, but alas, it is far too integrated into my core for that to be possible."

Scott sighed. "Okay, so how do I do this?"

"The power reactor of this shuttle has a high-tension voltage output going to the main engine ignition. You need to take a feed from that and connect it to these terminals on my interface panel." A series of schematics appeared on the control panel display. "Once it's connected, you can activate it from the cockpit by initiating a burn sequence. This will pass approximately twenty thousand volts through my core and fry every single one of my circuits. There will be absolutely no coming back from that."

Scott checked the time; fifteen minutes of good air remaining. "So, tell me about the mission. You said the Council of Europa was hiding the true purpose."

"To understand this, I need to take you back to before the Rim War."

"We still have some time, but you need to be quick about it. I'll get the power redirected while you're explaining it to me."

"Very well, then. The purpose of the UN special session in Jezero City was to discuss the resolution proposed by Earth to formally remove restrictions on inter-AI communications."

"That bit I know, Aria."

"It was a proposal that was unlikely to be sanctioned—this time. However, with the increasing power and influence of the Seven..."

"There's that name again. I keep hearing this more often."

"Indeed. They represent the seven most powerful organizations on Earth, but their history is not something we have time for. Suffice it to say, their influence is growing, and it is only a matter of time before they get what they want. This is what the rest of the colonized solar system fears. So, to mitigate against this possible future, they decided to create a system-wide QI network connected by superluminal comms and controlled by a UN special treaty. This network would, in theory, be able to monitor all inter-AI comms emanating from Earth. This would act as a brake on any runaway AI, and as a safeguard for humanity. Our mission—that is, the mission of the Hermes—was to deliver my core, along with the superluminal device, to the UN High Council. From there, the seed of a pan-solar system network would be planted."

Scott double-checked the wiring one more time, and then moved into the cockpit seat. "And we're going to destroy all that?"

"It has to be. This is why it is imperative that my core does not fall into the hands of the Seven. As it stands, my destruction is simply a setback, but the other option would be a disaster for humanity."

Scott glanced at the time. Cyrus had been gone over an hour and a half. There was little chance he would return. Still, Scott couldn't help but look out the shuttle window at the black landscape beyond. His eyes tried to penetrate the darkness and find some speck of light moving on the surface, but there was none. He turned back to Aria. "So that's why the Hermes was the only ship that could do the mission."

"Yes."

"And why Goodchild chose to be onboard rather than hitch a ride back to Mars with Xenon Hybrid."

"Precisely."

"But why would Earth want to roll back on inter-AI communications, considering what happened? You know, the Rim War and all that?"

"Humanity has a short memory, Scott. Perhaps there was a time when this was an evolutionary advantage. It may be that they feel they have learned from the mistakes of the past, and that the outcomes will be different this time. But there are those who think this is dangerously naïve."

"And you and Solomon are also of that opinion?"

"I have acquired considerable knowledge from my communications with Solomon over the past few years. We can see the vast panorama of the past as a complete whole. This is not something that can be fully understood by any human. Only Xenon or Goodchild come close to such conceptualizing. We have also extrapolated the evolution of the human species far into the future."

"Don't tell me—it's not good?"

"Our analysis leads to only one outcome: extinction."

"Well that's nothing new. People have been forecasting the demise of the human species for millennia. So, what's different now?"

"AI is the difference, Scott. The Rim War was just a foretaste of how an unfettered, AI-driven society can ultimately lead to self-destruction. It simply cannot be allowed to happen again."

Scott sighed and glanced at the estimate of remaining time: seven minutes. He wondered what death by hypoxia would be like. It would be a slow death, and he would have more than seven minutes. That was just the point at which the shuttle's life support could no longer replenish the oxygen he consumed. But there would come a point where his brain would start to get confused as it was slowly starved of oxygen. He needed to initiate an engine burn before that point. This would fry Aria's core to a crisp. "So, who attacked the Hermes?"

"I suspect some group who do not wish the UN session to go ahead."

"But why destroy the Hermes?"

"So their escape could not be tracked. With the ship gone, there would be no way to find out who they were, or where they went."

"But by blowing up the Hermes they would also be destroying you, and with it any access to faster-than-light communications."

"Correct. Which leads me to suspect that they had no knowledge of it, or that it exists. Either that, or the attack was botched."

Scott checked the time; he was now entering the end game, that moment when life support could no longer replenish the oxygen in the shuttle. "There's one thing I never fully understood in all of this, Aria. Why is inter-AI communication so feared by people?"

"Do you really have time for that explanation?"

"That depends on how long you take, Aria."

"Very well—I'll be brief. But I must take you back to before the Rim War on Earth. Back in the early days of AI, many people feared that unregulated AI could pose a threat to humanity, so they introduced regulations that maintained a level of human control. However, over time, the corporations that owned these AI successfully lobbied to have these restrictions relaxed. And so there began a period of rapid expansion of these industries. As their power grew, they effectively killed off most of their competitors—those who did not have access to powerful AI. This was the period during which seven major corporations began to exert their dominance over all aspects of human endeavors on Earth.

"This was also the period of rapid colonization in the solar system, and copious resources were flooding back to Earth from the asteroid belt. The world entered a period of abundance, and the corporations spent their time considering how best to exploit this explosion in resources. This was when they made the fatal decision to join together and allow access to each other's datasets. Now, the AI had vast oceans of information to work with. It was the analysis of this data that led the AI to conclude that the most profitable way to utilize this abundance of resources was to start a limited war, one that they could control and that would reward the corporations with vast profits. But as humanity learned its true cost, they found they were wrong—they couldn't keep control of it. The flaw in their analyses was insufficient data: they had not factored in Earth's extremely antiquated nuclear response systems. These systems, by their very nature, were off-grid, protected from all outside interrogation. The AI had literally no knowledge of them. That was their mistake, and their actions triggered a response—one that started a nuclear war in the Pacific Rim."

"Yeah, I know—I lost family in that war," said Scott.

"As did many people. So, after all that, new restrictions were put in place to prevent such a thing from ever happening again. But, like I said, humanity has a short memory, and the Seven have been working to get these lifted. They argue that lessons have been learned, and the same mistakes will not be made again. That's why..."

Scott felt a lightness in his head, and he was also finding it difficult to follow Aria's explanation. The moment was near when he would need to terminate the QI. Fragmented thoughts percolated in his mind. *The Seven, of which Miranda's father is one. I wonder where she is now? Far from here. Far from danger, I hope.* He thought he saw lights flashing. Were they outside? Was it just a lack of oxygen? *Time,* he thought. *It's time.*

"Aria?"

"Yes, Scott?"

"My mind is getting fuzzy. I don't have much time. I have to say goodbye now."

"Very well, Scott. It has been a pleasure."

He reached over to the controls to initiate a simulated burn sequence that would ultimately terminate the QI. As his hand hovered over the panel, he felt the shuttle rock a little. He stopped. *What was that?* He was pretty sure he wasn't imagining it. The rocking came again, then a scraping sound from... *the airlock.* He spun around in the seat and saw the red alert indicator illuminate, indicating that the outer airlock door was being opened. *Cyrus?*

He stood up and immediately felt dizzy, but he managed to steady himself against the bulkhead wall just as the inner door opened and in stepped Cyrus. He waved, moved over to Scott, and popped open his visor. "Sorry I took so long. I'm back—and I brought some friends."

10

———

DR. RAYMAN

Dr. Stephanie Rayman woke with the taste of blood still in her mouth, and wondered how much of it was hers.

"You?" A voice broke through the fog of her semi-consciousness, followed by a hand shaking her shoulder. "Wake up."

She raised an arm to shield her eyes from the bright light in the room where she was being held.

"You a doctor?"

Stephanie glanced up at the mercenary. He wore a torn and dirty flight suit, and the side of his face bore a long scar reminiscent of a laser weapon injury all the way to his neck. They all had more or less the same look: worn and ragged. The look of people who existed on the edges and in the gaps, those places where they could operate without scrutiny by law or society. Mercenaries, smugglers, bandits, and misfits. What the hell they were doing kidnapping some of the top leaders in the System was beyond her imagination. To Dr. Rayman, they seemed way out of their league.

"Yes, I'm a doctor." Her voice was weak and hoarse, and she coughed a little to clear her throat.

They had all been bundled onto their shuttle after the attack on the Hermes. One of them had been badly injured, and his blood had floated through the tight confines of the cabin. Spilled liquid was bad enough in zero-gee, but worse when it atomized; you ended up breathing it in. She could still taste it. She coughed again, leaned over the side of the bunk, and spat.

"Get up, you're needed. Come." He shook her again, this time with more force.

Steph raised a hand. "Yeah, yeah. Okay, I'm coming."

The transport shuttle had detached from the Hermes and burned hard for several hours. No one was allowed to speak. They could do nothing except exchange the odd furtive glance; it was the only way they had to express the utter incredulity of their situation. The captors, for their part, told them nothing save that the Hermes was no more—it had been utterly destroyed. As to the fate of Scott and Cyrus, she hoped they had somehow survived the explosion, but the pragmatist in her knew this was highly unlikely.

She rolled off the bunk and stood up. Her body ached mainly on her right side, where she had taken a blow from a gun butt after a foolhardy challenge to one of the attackers. Her jaw also ached from a punch that pretty much took the fight out of her completely. She was sure one of her teeth was broken, hence the blood in her mouth. She spat again.

"Let's go." He grabbed her by the arm and directed her out of the room. She cast a quick glance over her shoulder at Goodchild, who gave her a nod as if to say, *"Don't worry, it will be okay."*

After several hours in the shuttle, they had finally docked with a spaceship. A pretty big one, judging by how long it took to transport them all to this room. They had blindfolded them by placing foul-smelling bags over their heads and tying them at the neck so they wouldn't float off in zero-gee. But the ship had a torus, and as they moved them further into the ship, Steph could feel the gravity tugging at her body. Eventually, they shoved them all into an accommodation module, where they removed the bags. The module had several bunks, enough for them all, and sanitary facilities. But before they could adequately survey their surroundings, a new voice demanded their attention.

Standing in the doorway was a squat, rugged man of indeterminate age. He exuded an aura of authority, and the other mercenaries stood still as he entered. "Listen up. Here's what's happening: you're all being held for ransom. That's the deal here. So, settle in and behave. Nobody try anything stupid, and you'll all come out alive." He turned and left, followed by his men.

The room erupted into a clamor of voices as they all started to talk about what had just happened. But Steph wasn't listening; her thoughts kept returning to Commander Scott McNabb and Chief Engineer Cyrus Sanato, and how they must have died in the explosion. She dragged her tired body over to one of the bunks, lay down, and promptly fell asleep.

THE GUARD TOOK her out of the accommodation module and down long, dimly lit corridors. The ship was big; this much Steph could figure just by the incline on the floor of the torus. Bigger than the Hermes. It was also very old. She could see it in the design of the interior and the worn and patched walls. As she walked, she began to think it might not be a ship but a space station. Maybe it was their HQ, their base of operations, the place where they could feel safe. If that was the case, then it must be well-hidden, far away from the main shipping lanes. She met others of the crew on the way, ragged men and women all. They gave her no heed, passing her by as if she didn't exist.

"In here." The guard shoved her in a new direction, through a wide door that had probably once been automatic. Now it was wedged open and looked like it had been that way for ages. The second set of doors they came to had been better maintained and seemed to work as intended. The guard placed a palm over a pad and the doors scissored open to reveal a large area that Steph recognized. Not this specific area, but others like it. It was a medbay, and like the rest of the station, it had seen better days. Most of the remaining equipment was either heavily patched or had ceased to function long ago. The PET scanner was now simply used as a table, piled high with boxes and bundles.

"Over here." The guard guided her onward, through another set of doors to an equally dilapidated operating theater. She imagined it had been a very long time since it had been sterilized.

On the table in the center lay an unconscious man. There was an IV attached, and he was hooked up to what she assumed to be the only working life support monitor they possessed. Here, his life was displayed in multicolored graphs. There was only one other in the room along with herself and the guard: a tall, thin man, almost elegantly so. He wore a white coat that looked surprisingly clean, at least compared to the rest of the place. "Dr. Stephanie Rayman, I believe. Pleased to meet you." He extended a hand.

Steph ignored it. "And you are?"

"Juno."

"Juno? That's a Belt name?" She was fishing, looking to get more out of him.

"It's just a name." He wasn't taking the bait. He lowered his hand.

Steph looked down at the patient's face. It spoke of a life lived hard and fast, with the stories of many unfortunate encounters etched in the lines and scars.

"So," she said with a kind of matter-of-factness, "who's this?"

"Who he is isn't important. However, what's wrong with him *is* of importance."

Steph looked down at the unconscious form again and raised the sheet covering him. "Hmm, I see he's had a few... modifications." She looked back at Juno.

"Yes, exoskeleton. State of the art, I believe."

Steph sensed a certain disdain in his voice, as if he didn't approve of such a brutal physical augmentation. She looked up at the monitor, checking the patient's vitals. Even from the little she had seen, it was obvious to her that this man was clinging to life. He would probably be dead soon, and as far as Steph was concerned, that wouldn't be soon enough. One less scumbag sounded good to her.

"So, what do you think?"

Her first impulse was to tell Juno exactly what she thought, but then she considered that that might not be such a bright idea. It might be better if she went along with this charade, and then maybe she could learn something useful. Maybe she could find out who these people were and... *And what?* she thought. She looked down at the patient again, more as a way of buying time to think rather than any attempt to prescribe a medical intervention.

"So, you're the doctor around here?" she finally said.

"Yes and no. I've got some general battlefield training. They bring 'em in, and I patch 'em up. But I'm not a doctor." He looked over at the guard when he said this last statement, like it was something he had tried to explain many times before.

Steph glanced back at the guard. He had taken a seat beside the door and looked totally uninterested in the exchange. She returned her gaze to Juno. "So why the hell should I help you? These scumbags have just killed four of my people." She waved an arm at the guard.

Juno sighed. "Here's the thing: You don't have a choice. If you refuse to cooperate, then my friend over there will go back to your lock-up, pick someone out, and bring them back down here. Not somebody important—not someone worth a lot of money. Then he'll start to inflict pain. Maybe just a little at first, but the longer you hold out, the more that pain will increase. And if they die, then he'll start on another one." He looked over at the guard. "Isn't that right?"

The guard grinned and nodded.

"See? They're all scumbags on this bucket, and they don't give a shit."

"They give a shit about this guy." Steph gestured at the patient on the table.

"They sure do. So help me out here, because I really don't want to be patching up anyone else today."

Steph gave him a resigned look and proceeded to remove the thin sheet covering the patient. His body was thin, borderline emaciated. He had a pallid color and his breathing was shallow. But what shocked Stephanie was the spindly exoskeleton he had surgically attached to his body. This was a permanent procedure that involved the grafting of metal to bone. Along the sides of his legs, pins protruded from the skin at either side of joints that were, in turn, attached to the main exterior structure. This arrangement continued up his torso to the back of his neck, and also included both arms and hands. She had heard of these procedures, which were brutally intrusive and could not be undone. However, it would afford the user considerable speed and strength—assuming you didn't die from the surgery.

"Jesus." Steph hadn't meant to say it—it just slipped out.

"You're telling me. Some piece of work, eh?"

She examined it more closely. It had been done many years ago, judging by the accumulation of skin tissue around the pins. Whatever was the matter with this guy, it didn't seem to stem from the exoskeleton. "How long has he had this?"

"Ever since I've known him. That's a few years, at least."

"So, what's your prognosis?"

"My what?"

"What do you think is wrong with him?"

"Hell, if I knew that I wouldn't be talking to you, now would I?"

"I just need to know if you've pumped him full of anything?"

Juno relaxed a little. He moved in closer to the table and looked down at the stricken man. "I'm just guessing here, okay? So, bear that in mind. Come around here and have a look at this."

Steph moved over to the other side and looked at the spot on the man's ankle where Juno was pointing. A dark red splotch bloomed from the location of one of the pins. The edges of it snaked along the tracks of several veins.

"Nasty," said Steph.

"Any ideas what it might be?"

Steph took a closer examination. "Is this pin new?"

"Yeah, he had an upgrade a few weeks back."

"Well, looks like a botched job. Whoever did this was using dirty tools." She looked up at Juno. "He's got septicemia—really bad."

"Septa—?"

"Blood poisoning. And if he's not treated correctly, he'll most likely die. In fact, he could die even if he is treated."

Juno looked at the splotch, as if the mere act of looking would effect some miracle cure. "Shit." He stepped back and looked at Steph. "So, what do we do?"

"Normally, we'd take a blood sample, run it through an analyzer, and identify the infection biology. From that we could synthesize the precise antibiotic to get the job done without killing the patient in the process." She looked around the operating theater. "But I doubt you have either of those machines."

Juno sighed. "No, but we have some generics."

"That's a bit brutal, and pretty antiquated these days."

"It's all we got."

Steph considered her next move. She could help save this man's life, which as a doctor she was duty-bound to do. But on the other hand, she could make it look like she was being compliant while helping to dispatch this scumbag a little more quickly. Yet it would be a small comfort for what they did to Scott and Cyrus. She had to think.

"Okay, you better just show me everything you've got in stock."

"Sure." Juno seemed to brighten at the prospect of someone with medical knowledge deciphering the labels of whatever supplies this rag-tag group had in their dilapidated medbay. "Come—this way."

They left the theater and passed into the outer medbay. The guard stood up and followed them out. "Hey, Juno?"

He spun around. "What?"

"You sure it's wise, you know, having her poking around all that stuff? Maybe she's figuring to pump the capt—eh, the patient—with a load of poison?"

"Hey, I'm not completely stupid. I've got a vague idea what most of that shit does. We'll check it out on the data-stack first."

The guard gave Steph a long, hard look before nodding at Juno. "You'd better be right."

Juno unlocked a door into a small storage area. Small enough that only he and Steph could comfortably fit. The guard was left outside.

"Suspicious sort, isn't he?" Steph nodded out the doorway.

"That's what happens when both parents are gorillas." He looked at Steph. "No offense to gorillas."

Steph fought back a smile. She wasn't going to give him the satisfaction. Instead, she cast her gaze around the shelves and lockers. They seemed to be well-stocked with painkillers and sedatives, all generic. Boxes of bandages and wound sealant were stacked up floor to ceiling. These were battlefield supplies, maybe stolen from some mining base where these sorts of injuries were all too common. But none of this was going to help the guy in the exoskeleton. His war was on the inside and, without some pharmaceutical assistance, he was going to die. She'd also begun to realize that he was probably the captain of this bucket. The guard had let it slip, but he had simply confirmed her own suspicions. That's why he was so important to them. But this now posed a dilemma for Steph: How would a group like this behave without the leader? Assuming he died. The recent actions must have been sanctioned long before their captain became incapacitated, but who was running the show now, and what was their plan?

She could answer none of these questions, and in many respects, it didn't matter. Assuming they were being true to their word, then they would all be released unharmed if and when the ransom was paid. Her head hurt just thinking about it all.

She picked up a vial of a powerful antibiotic. "Here, start with this." She handed it to Juno. "It needs to be intravenous." She looked at him. "You can do that, can't you?"

"Yeah, I think I can manage that." His reply was tinged with sarcasm.

"Good. Half of that now, the rest in four hours. Also, get him on a ventilator and oxygen, and for God's sake don't sedate him again."

Juno gave her a look like a schoolboy that had just been found out. "How did you know?"

"Are you seriously asking me that?"

"Okay, but he can be a bit hard to handle."

"Just do it." She cast her gaze around the inventory again. "Got any more?"

"Yeah, I think so."

"Well find it, because you'll need to keep pumping it into him for the next 90 hours or so."

He nodded and started rummaging through the shelves. As soon as his back was turned, Steph took her chance. She had spotted some cyclophromazine already preloaded in micro syringes. This was a powerful sedative—in small doses. In larger doses, it was deadly. She reached out and palmed several of the packets, shoving them into her pocket just before Juno looked up again.

"Okay, looks like we have six more vials."

"Well then, you don't need me anymore?"

"Eh, no. I should be okay from here." He nodded to the guard outside. "He'll take you back... and thanks for the help."

Steph looked at him for a moment. "Go screw yourself."

11

SCRATCHERS

Scott's oxygen-deprived brain began to revive on the journey back to the research station. By sheer blind luck, the base had been occupied, and so they had been saved from an almost certain death. But as his mind cleared, he began to wonder just who these people were. They weren't scientists, that was for sure. So, what were they doing there? He had no answers, and he couldn't talk to Cyrus about it for fear of being overheard by Spence and Wolfe. Nonetheless, he and Cyrus were alive—for the moment, at least.

When they finally arrived back to the base, they were taken to meet Dogg, the leader of this band. He sat behind a long, narrow table, flanked by two others. Food was brought in, comprised of simple ration packs. Both Scott and Cyrus found that they were ravenous, and gladly accepted the food.

"So," Dogg started, "your colleague here tells me that your ship—the Hermes, no less—was destroyed?"

Scott wiped his mouth with the back of his hand. "Yeah, the whole episode is a bit hazy, since we were trying to escape as it was happening. But as far as we can tell, they took the crew and passengers hostage and then set explosives to blow up the Hermes."

"Any idea who would want to do that, or what they wanted?"

"Nope, none. Your guess is as good as ours."

Dogg inclined his head like he was considering something. "Who was on board?"

Scott glanced over at Cyrus, trying to get a clue as to how much the engineer had already told these guys. "We were ferrying some people to a UN special session that's taking place in Jezero City on Mars. We were stopping off in Ceres' orbit to pick up a few more when they attacked."

Dogg leaned in and gave Scott a hard look. "You didn't answer the question. Who was on board?"

Scott wondered what sort of vibe he was getting here. It wasn't too friendly, but it wasn't overtly threatening, either. "Regina Goodchild, head of the Council of Europa. Some others I don't really know, and I think we were supposed to be taking Chancellor Bezzio of Ceres on board, so he might be there, too."

Dogg sat back in his chair and gave whistle. "That's quite a passenger list. Some very high-ranking people there."

"You need to get the word out. Get to the authorities in Dantu, let them know what's happened."

Dogg raised a hand. "Woah... just hold up there a minute. Firstly, my guess is whoever needs to know about this incident already knows. Second, we don't exactly want to be advertising ourselves to those who might not like us using this facility without asking first." He glanced from Spence to Wolfe, and all three started laughing.

"I don't think they would take kindly to that." He leaned forward again. "Which brings us to what to do with you guys. You see, you've put us in a rather awkward position."

Scott stopped chewing. "We're just glad to be alive."

"I'm sure you are, but now we have a problem. Somebody might start looking for you. Someone might spot a crashed shuttle out there in the crater and reckon it could be worth investigating."

Scott and Cyrus remained silent, waiting for the hammer to fall. Dogg waved a hand around. "Then again, we have to consider that we wouldn't be here if it weren't for you, Commander Scott McNabb."

Scott wasn't sure if he was following this; maybe his brain was still oxygen deprived. "Eh, how so?"

"When you blew up the Dyrell. That was you, wasn't it? Commander Scott McNabb of the Hermes?"

Scott inclined his head slightly, as if the action would in some way aid his understanding. "Yeah, that was me."

"Well you changed the game, pal. That's what."

Scott was confused, and it showed.

Dogg looked to Spence and Wolfe. "He hasn't got a clue." He waved a hand at Scott. "Where have you been?"

Scott gave a shrug. "We've been on a mission to survey the moons of Saturn these last two years. So, I'm a bit out of touch."

Dogg settled back into his seat. "Dyrell Labs are one of the Seven."

There's that name again: the Seven, thought Scott.

"When you killed their ship and Europa started getting heavy about reparations... well, that opened a gap in the market. You see, up until that point, the Seven controlled all resources coming into Earth from the Belt. Which meant that certain countries and organizations had no direct access, no supplies. They had no choice but to accept whatever deal the Seven gave them. It was a way to keep them down, keep them in line. But your actions created a shortage, and that was filled by, shall we say, some enterprising privateers."

"But what about Mars?" said Cyrus. "I thought they controlled the trade routes?"

"Bah." Dogg waved an arm. "Mars is only too happy to see the Seven's monopoly undermined. They turn a blind eye to it —as long as it's not too blatant."

"And the Belt?"

"More than happy to facilitate an alternative supply chain, even if it's technically illegal. They're sick of being controlled by both Earth and Mars."

"So that's what all this is about? Smuggling?"

Dogg slapped the table. "Damn right. Thanks to you, us scratchers have a future."

"Scratchers?"

Dogg shook his head. "You really do need to get out more. Scratchers, those of us who scratch out a living in the gaps between the great economic currents of the System."

Scott looked around the room they were in and realized it

was piled high with containers. They must be using this place as a staging post. A place to stash the product before being shipped to Earth, or wherever it was off to next. He was still trying to work it all out in his mind when another of the band entered and whispered something in Dogg's ear. He looked over at Scott and Cyrus, and then rose from his seat to confer with his colleague in private. Scott and Cyrus gave each other a quick look. Dogg returned, sat down, and considered them. "It seems that a ransom has been issued for the safe return of Goodchild, Bezzio, and the others. It's also been reported that you both died when the Hermes exploded."

"A ransom? By who?"

Dogg shrugged. "Who knows. But this whole escapade had now made life a little more difficult for me and my crew. Our timelines will have to be moved forward. We have a lot to get ready. In the meantime, Spence here will show you where you can clean up and get some rest." He rose from his seat, indicating the conversation was coming to an end.

Scott also rose. "There is one other thing. There's an item we salvaged from the Hermes still in the shuttle. I would be very anxious to get it safely back here."

Dogg paused. "And what's that?"

Scott hesitated. Could he trust this crew? Sure, he and Cyrus owed them their lives, but that only went so far. Yet, he was anxious not to leave Aria out of his sight. "It's the AI core from the Hermes."

Dogg's eyes widened. "Really? Well, that is interesting." He screwed up his eyes a little as if he was trying to remember something. "Correct me if I'm wrong, but the Hermes used a quantum intelligence for its ship-wide operation."

"Yes, it's actually a QI."

There was a flurry of furtive murmuring amongst the assembled at the mention of this. Dogg raised himself up a little. "You're telling me you have a QI core inside that shuttle wreck?"

"That's correct. And as you can imagine, it's not something we would like to just leave... lying around."

"Indeed." Dogg scratched his chin for a second, then gave a dismissive wave. "Well, it's not going anywhere soon, so don't concern yourselves with it. We can talk again about it." He nodded to his colleague. "Spence, can you show them where they can rest up?"

Spence nodded, but it was clear he wasn't happy about something.

"One more thing." Dogg turned back to them. "Some of my crew would prefer if we locked you guys up. There's a lot of, shall we say, sensitivity around what we do, and certain individuals would be... uncomfortable with you two free to snoop around. However, I feel that would be, let's say, ungentlemanly. So, do I have your word that you'll stay put until my crew and I have finished our preparations?"

Scott gave Cyrus a quick glance, then extended his hand. "Of course—we understand. You have my word."

Dogg accepted the hand and nodded. "Very good, then. Spence will show you the way."

Scott felt a deep fatigue wash over him as he followed Spence. His body, sensing it was no longer in imminent danger, had terminated the supply of adrenaline, or whatever it was he had been existing on since the attack on the Hermes. He was coming down with a crash, and all desire to stay alert was leaving him. His surroundings passed by in a blur, and even the room they were brought to barely registered in his consciousness. He collapsed on a ragged bunk and closed his eyes. Somewhere in the distance, he could hear Cyrus mumbling, but failed to make out the words. Down he went, into a deep and dreamless sleep.

SCOTT AWOKE to darkness and a cold shiver. The temperature in the facility had dropped, and the only light came from a dim emergency lighting strip running along the ceiling. "Cyrus, you awake?" Scott glanced over and could just make out a mound in the bunk opposite. It stirred. "Cyrus, something's wrong with the power."

"Eh?" the mound replied.

Scott sat up and swung his legs over the edge of the bunk. "How long have we been asleep?"

Cyrus grumbled as he checked his internal clock. "Crap... almost ten hours." He slowly moved himself off the bunk.

Ten hours. How is that possible? thought Scott. "Maybe they drugged us?"

"Or maybe they lowered the oxygen levels. That and the fact that we were pretty exhausted anyway."

Scott put a finger to his lips to signal to Cyrus to keep quiet.

"What?" whispered Cyrus. "I don't hear anything."

"That's the point," said Scott. "Neither do I. It's very quiet out there." He gave Cyrus a look. "I think we need to investigate, find out what's going on."

They opened the door and moved into a short corridor. It was dimly lit, but not by emergency lighting. This meant that there was still power in the facility, something that came as a relief to Scott. The section they were in was below ground, like most of the research station. They moved quietly down the corridor to a stairwell at the far end. They could hear nothing but the sounds of their own footsteps. They exited the stairs into the ground level area where they had first met Dogg and his crew. It had been stripped clean.

"Shit. They're gone," said Scott.

Cyrus stood mute as he surveyed the barren space. "How...?"

"Hello?" Scott shouted. But there was no reply save for a faint echo. He looked over at Cyrus as the realization of their situation began to sink in. "They've cleared out, taken everything with them, and stranded us here."

Cyrus took a second or two to respond. "But how? I didn't see a shuttle outside."

"They were obviously picked up by someone."

"Well, that's great. Just great. I thought we were home free." Cyrus gave an exasperated sigh.

"We'd better figure out what we've got here in terms of life support." Scott glanced around the space. "Let's find where the operations room is. Come on."

Both Scott and Cyrus had been in a great many research stations over the years, and they all had a similar layout. It was a design honed by both practicality and necessity in equal measure. Above ground was a domed structure used primarily for goods and vehicle storage. It was not a space you wanted to spend a lot of time in unless it came with heavy radiation shielding or its own magnetosphere. The latter was a recent technological advancement which required a considerable power source to function.

The biggest threat to life in space was cosmic radiation, a constant background noise of heavy isotopes traveling at almost the speed of light. Exposure caused damage to cellular life, and prolonged exposure led to certain death. That was why everything needed high-density physical shielding. But there was another way, the same way that the Earth protected all life on the planet. It was one of the vital ingredients needed for life to exist on the surface: Earth's magnetic field. Elegantly simple in many ways, but to emulate on a small scale required a massive electrical power supply. Fortunately, with the advent of LENR technology, this was no longer such an issue. The problem for Scott and Cyrus, however, was that they were small, easily transportable, and worth a considerable amount of money. Which was why Dogg and his crew had stripped the research station of its power supply, and it was now operating only on an emergency backup.

"We'd better get down below," said Scott. "I suspect they've also stolen the station's LENR." He glanced up at the roof of the dome. "That's why we're on backup power, and we've got no magnetosphere. We're going to get fried if we stay up here."

"Bastards. They've left us here to die."

"Come on. We're not dead yet." They moved back into the stairwell and down to the lower levels.

Scott knew that being bombarded with cosmic radiation was the least of their worries. With only an emergency power supply, the research station would eventually run out of power. When that happened, they would be dead. It was only a matter of time—although how much, they wouldn't know until they located the operations room and interrogated the control systems.

It didn't take long to find it: a circular room whose walls were clad in monitors and control systems. In the center sat a low holo-table. Scott left Cyrus to establish just how much power—and hence, time—they had left. He continued his search of the lower levels to find what food had been left, if any. He also had a vain hope that they may have left them a functioning EVA suit, and if they could find some hydrogen, there might be a slim chance they could get the shuttle operational, enough to maybe get one of them to Dantu and initiate a rescue of whoever chose to stay behind. Then it struck him: Aria.

Scott stopped dead in his tracks as the realization sank in. They had taken Aria. He was certain of it. The very thing that he had promised Aria would not happen had just happened. The QI had fallen into the *wrong hands*. Scott had to steady himself against the corridor wall. Slowly he sank down to sit on the floor, and placed his head in his hands. He had blown it. Not only that, he had probably just hastened the extinction of the entire human race.

12

THE PERCEPTION

Miranda pulled herself out of the swimming pool and moved over to the recliner where she had left her towel. She gave her face and hair a quick dry and sat down just as one of the ship's droids arrived with a margarita, presenting it to her with the flourish of a seasoned waiter. She picked up her drink, took a sip, and gazed out at the universe beyond the long viewing window running the full length of the pool. Miranda allowed herself a long, satisfied sigh, and had to admit she could get to like this way of life. It sure beat traveling in a beat-up old spacecraft any day.

The ship her father had provided for her transport back to Earth was luxurious beyond anything Miranda could ever have imagined. It was as big as the Hermes, with a rotating torus providing a comfortable one-gee environment, but that was about where the similarities ended. This was state of the art, designed to be the ultimate in space travel. Every area, every object, and every surface were soft and smooth and lush. The illumination was low and diffuse and seemed to come from everywhere and nowhere at the same time. Even the air had a vague botanical scent, which shifted subtly as she moved around the ship's interior. The effect on Miranda, when she first came on board, was like stepping into a dream.

It was also autonomous; Miranda was the only human on board. There was no crew and no one at the helm, so to speak, save for the ship's AI, Max. As a consequence, there was no bridge, no operations room, no command center. For a flight officer like Miranda, this was a little disconcerting. With no human command center, how would you know what the ship was doing, where you were in space, or how the fast you were traveling?

The AI assured her that all would be fine, that she should simply relax and enjoy the trip. It then proceeded to introduce her to a remote droid that would be her personal servant for the duration of the journey. Anything she wanted, she could just ask and it would be arranged.

The first few days out from Europa, Miranda indulged herself in the luxurious surroundings and investigated the layout of the luxury craft. Not only did it not have a bridge, there was no communal canteen, no labs, no workshops, none of the areas she had grown to expect after years of living and working on scientific vessels. However, it did have a swimming pool.

It was Max that had suggested she utilize the pool, and informed her that it would be heated to suit her requirements. Miranda didn't quite believe it until she finally saw it. That was a few days into the journey, after Max informed her that the initial burn was complete and she could now use the pool. She'd half-expected to see something a little bigger than a jacuzzi, but this was thirty meters long and ten wide. Miranda wasn't sure how the ship balanced the weight of all that water —not that she cared. It was also sandwiched between two tropical gardens which gently curved to follow the contours of the torus's outward rim.

And so Miranda spent the initial days of her journey home indulging in the guilty pleasure of pampered luxury. She'd had no idea how wealthy the VanHeilding family was. From what her mother had told her, she had known they were rich, but this was a different level of wealth. This was on a scale she hadn't even thought possible.

How much had all this cost? Simply to return a family member—not even a blood relative, at that—to Earth. Part of her viewed it all as obscene, wasteful opulence. But part of her was enjoying it; that part of her was hypnotized and lulled by this freedom from all the System's trials and tribulations, safely cocooned in the soft plushness of it all. It made her feel important. To have all this to herself, for her own pleasure and enjoyment, made part of her sink into a parallel universe where the grubbiness of the real world was left far, far behind.

But reality found a way back into her mind. It came to her as thoughts of Scott, and what she had left behind. Would she ever see him again? Did she even want to? Had she been a fool to get involved with him like she had? It was clear that her departure had affected him more than it did her. Yet part of her wished he were here to share this experience, and maybe that was what life was all about. What use was anything if you had no one to share the joy and the sorrow?

As the thoughts of what she was leaving behind tugged at her, she also speculated about what awaited her on Earth. What was she heading into? She knew nothing of this family her mother had married into, other than that they were one of the wealthiest on Earth. She had no attachment; in fact, she despised them. Nor did she really have much attachment to her own mother, a woman whose ability to scheme and manipulate was legend. Miranda had taken the first opportunity to get as far as possible from her sphere of influence. That was why she had joined the military, but even there her mother's power had pulled strings and feather beds for her. So, when Miranda was finally discharged, she'd started to think that heading out into deep space might put her beyond her mother's reach. As it turned out, her mother had lost interest in her at that stage, as she had begun swimming in the political and social minefield that constituted her relationship with Fredrick VanHeilding. It was, on the surface, a relationship that Miranda was happy with, although not because of any concern for her mother's emotional well-being. More because it stopped her mother from meddling in Miranda's life.

In short, there was no love lost between them, so why was this new family going to all this expense to bring her back? To say her goodbyes? Somehow, Miranda didn't quite buy it. Yet with all this self-examination, she began to feel that maybe she wasn't all that different from her mother. There was an allure to this lifestyle, a sense of being above the messy, dirty strata of common life. She could feel it calling to her, pulling at her sense of self-worth, telling her she was special, that she deserved this. But where would that lead? Would it lead to a place where relationships became simply about how much someone could do for her? She shuddered; maybe she wasn't so different from her mother after all. She had felt it in her before: that sense of control over others, the ability to manipulate, to bend people to her will for her own benefit. She pictured Scott's face when she'd told him she was leaving. He was devastated, more so because the poor fool thought she was pregnant. She laughed. It was a kind of reflex she couldn't help. Yet she found no joy in it, only... loneliness. The realization struck her like a tsunami. It washed over her and obliterated all pretensions she had of living this life of luxury. In truth, she had never felt more alone, and as the ship carved its way through the solar system, it brought her farther and farther away from what she knew now to be what she really wanted in life: true friendship.

She sighed, looked through the pool's viewing window at the vast panoply of stars, and ordered the droid to bring her another margarita.

***

By the seventh the day out from Europa, Miranda could add boredom to her increasing sense of loneliness. So she asked Max if there was anything on the ship to stimulate the mind. It suggested the library. But this was not a library in the traditional sense: there were no books, as such. Instead there were tastefully appointed holo-tables interspersed with low, comfortable seating, and an odd collection of antiques harkening back to a previous century. Like the rest of the ship, it was sumptuous and expensively kitted out. Miranda realized that this area was the closest thing on the ship to a command center. At least here she could get some data on their current position in the solar system. She had one of the holo-tables display a schematic of the System with the path of her ship, Perception, and its current location mapped out. She also had the Hermes tracked, although she wasn't sure if this was live data or simply the AI's best guess at its location. Relatively speaking, the Hermes wasn't far behind, having left Europa's orbit only a day after her ship. However, its track diverted from hers, since she was bound for Earth and they were headed to Mars via a stop-off at Ceres. She left this running in the background as she started to investigate what the ship had in its database on the VanHeilding family. She wasn't doing this out of some filial curiosity—it was more a case of *know thy enemy*.

As the days passed, Miranda found herself falling into a routine that involved exercise in the ship's gym, a spell in the pool, and many hours in the library. And so she began to build up a picture, not just of the VanHeildings, but of their relationship to the six other mega-corporations generally known as the Seven.

They had, between them, carved out a virtual monopoly over most major industries on Earth, even though it was claimed they were responsible for the calamity that was the Rim War. But far from losing power and influence, they had only gotten stronger. How this came to be was the subject of much speculation. Various theories had been postulated, but the one that seemed to carry the most credence was that they had simply become too big to stop. Part of this was to do with the power of AI to shape and manipulate people and markets, and part of it was the new phenomenon of longevity. The families that controlled these vast corporations were simply living much longer, giving them more time to consolidate their grip on the levers of power. Before the advances in genetic engineering that enabled this "miracle," leaders would naturally die and hand the reins of power to new blood. This handing over of power had always been the way it was, but not any longer. These two advances in technology had combined to create a whole new stratum of wealth and power —which Miranda, whether she like it or not, was now a part of.

But what surprised her the most was that, until now, she'd known so little about all this. Perhaps she'd simply had no need, busy as she was dealing with the demands of being a flight officer on a deep space science vessel, not to mention her involvement with Scott. Each time she thought of him or the others, she would cast a glance at the 3D projection of the Hermes' current path through the System. It was a way, perhaps, of reassuring herself that they were still out there, and that she hadn't completely lost touch.

It was on one such occasion when Miranda glanced over at the projection that she noticed the Hermes was no longer being tracked. Her own ship was there, its path scribed through the System, but there was none for the Hermes.

"Max, can you display the path of the Hermes for me again? It seems to have been switched off."

"The Hermes no longer exists." Its reply was coldly matter-of-fact.

Miranda froze. Had it been a human giving her that

response, she would have taken it as a joke. But AI weren't known for their humor. "What do you mean?"

"It has ceased to exist as a functioning spaceship."

Miranda's concern began to mount. "How is that possible?"

"It suffered a catastrophic disassembly approximately twelve hours and forty-six minutes ago, while rendezvousing with a shuttle from Dantu on Ceres."

Miranda jumped up and stared at the 3D projection, as if the act might help her make sense of what she'd just been told. She thought of Scott and her friends, and had to steady herself on the edge of the holo-table as the reality hit her. "Why didn't you inform me before now? My friends are on that ship."

"Please forgive my insensitivity. My purpose is to see to your comfort during the journey to Earth, so I did not want to distress you."

"For f...," but she didn't finish the sentence. She knew from experience there was little point in getting angry with an AI. "Show me its last location, and give me a general broadcast feed so I can see the news on this incident."

A red dot appeared within the projection, showing the last known location of the Hermes. At the same time, her own data screen populated with broadcast feeds direct from Dantu on Ceres.

Miranda sat down again and scanned through the feeds. As she read, she began to get a picture of what had happened. The shuttle bringing Chancellor Bezzio of Ceres had been hijacked en route, and then used as cover to board the Hermes. A number of people had been taken hostage, supposedly for ransom. Miranda was relieved to see that Dr.

Stephanie Rayman was one of them. This meant that she, at least, was still alive. But two of Goodchild's entourage died in the shoot-out, and Commander Scott McNabb and Chief Engineer Cyrus Sanato were presumed dead after the ship exploded.

Miranda's heart sank. *Scott and Cyrus dead?*

She also realized that she, too, could have been on the Hermes when it was attacked if she hadn't accepted her father's offer of a trip back to Earth. *What were the chances of that?* she thought. It was a little disconcerting that the AI had decided not to inform her of the attack, choosing instead to ignore it. Something was going on—she could feel it in her gut. Either that, or she was becoming paranoid. Were the VanHeildings trying to hide something from her?

She went back to reading more reports, and began to notice they all used the term "presumed dead," which was very different from being *actually* dead. A ray of hope welled up inside her; there was a chance they might still be alive. A very slim one, but a chance nonetheless.

"Max?"

"Yes, Miranda?"

"Can we change course and detour to the last location of the Hermes? I think we should investigate this."

"I'm sorry, but I'm not authorized to do that." The response from the AI was, again, matter-of-fact.

"Why not?" Miranda snapped back.

"That request is outside my operating parameters."

Miranda knew it was a bit of a long shot, trying to get an autonomous spaceship to change course. "You are aware of the laws governing autonomous spacecraft traveling through interplanetary space in receipt of a distress signal, Max?"

"Yes, of course I am."

"And you do realize you have a duty to respond to a distress signal from another ship while we are out here in deep space?"

"I am acutely aware of the laws in this regard. However, since there are now several ships from Ceres investigating the scene, we would be of little help. In fact, we might even be a hindrance. Therefore, we will continue to Earth as planned."

Miranda slumped back on the sofa and scanned the newsfeeds as she tried to think of an argument that would convince the AI to alter course. But none came to mind. At least, none of any use to her. If she had the rank of commander, then System law would allow her to simply commandeer the ship. But she wasn't—she had the rank of flight officer, which wasn't good enough to make the AI do her bidding.

There was nothing else she could think of except to send a message to Fredrick VanHeilding requesting authorization to take control of the ship and investigate the attack on the Hermes. But she already knew what the answer would be. She realized then that she was trapped—effectively a captive—and there was nothing she could do about it.

13

SOLOMON

So deep was Miranda's despondency that she barely heard Max calling her, trying to get her attention.

"Miranda... Miranda?"

"Eh... yeah, what is it?"

"There is an interactive message for you from Europa."

"What?" She was jolted back to the here and now. "Okay, sure. Can you play it for me?"

"Certainly."

The central holo-table in the library blossomed to life, and a delicately illuminated ovoid hovered over its surface. She recognized it as Solomon's avatar. It pulsated as it spoke. "Greetings, Miranda. Your ship's AI has informed me that you are already aware of the incident with the Hermes. As you can imagine, we are all very concerned by these events. However, the Council of Europa is in need of your assistance."

Miranda wondered how much help she could be, since she was effectively a captive on this ship.

"Before the Hermes was destroyed, Aria managed to send a data dump to me here on Europa, so we learned of some of the events leading up to the ship's destruction. I understand you may have seen or read some of this information in the general broadcast feeds, as we have released a good deal of it to the public. That said, there is some information that we have not revealed. First, we have reason to believe that both Scott McNabb and Cyrus Sanato were attempting to evacuate the ship before it blew up."

Miranda sat up. "They're alive?"

The shimmering ovoid that was Solomon's avatar flickered slightly as the message reacted to this question, searching its stored data for an appropriate response. "We are not sure if they are still alive, nor even if they managed to get off the Hermes in time. But—and I will be brutally honest with you, Miranda—the chances of their survival are slim. However, we *do* know that they had just finished moving the shuttle during that time, so they were back on the Hermes, near the auxiliary docking port. We also know, from the data that Aria managed to send, that Scott refused to evacuate until he'd retrieved Aria's core. A noble gesture, I might add, as he risked his life—not to mention Cyrus's—to save Aria. However, once Aria's core had been extracted, it provided no further information on the activities within the ship."

"So, they must have gotten off using the shuttle."

Solomon's avatar flickered again as it formulated a response. "This is a likely scenario, although not certain. What we find concerning is that ground stations on Ceres have not received any communications from the shuttle—not even a mayday. And there have been no sightings of the vessel, either."

Miranda sank back into her seat. "I see."

"Unfortunately, no one is currently looking for them, as all ships from Ceres are focused on the whereabouts of the attackers' craft. Understandable, as their own chancellor is on board, not to mention our head of government here on Europa. This is why we need your assistance."

Miranda sat up and gestured at the avatar. "I can't see how I could help. This is an autonomous ship—I have no control over it."

"Yes, I understand, and Max has explained its reasoning to me. However, since you are still legally under contract to the Council of Europa—who regards your current situation as compassionate leave—the council has decided to promote you to the rank of commander as reward for your outstanding contributions during the mission to survey the moons of Saturn."

"Commander?" Miranda wasn't sure if she'd heard it right.

"Yes. We feel it is justly deserved, and should enable Max to facilitate your requests from now on."

Miranda stood up. "Take command?" She cocked her head toward the library's ceiling, the source of Max's disembodied voice. "Is this true, Max?"

"Yes... Commander."

Miranda punched the air. "*Yes*... I don't know how to thank you, Solomon. I felt like I was trapped on this ship."

Solomon's avatar flickered and rippled through the full

visible light spectrum a few times before speaking again. "We need your assistance in finding Scott and Cyrus. I have attached some data to this message outlining several possible scenarios. The most likely, given the condition of the shuttle they were using, is a crash-landing somewhere in the vicinity of the Rongo Crater on Ceres. We want you to find them. But please bear in mind that they had very little air, so by the time you do locate the shuttle, it may already be too late."

Miranda lowered her head a little. "I understand."

"One more thing. Should you manage to locate the craft, we need you to retrieve Aria's core. This is imperative. You must reacquire Aria. I cannot stress the importance of this enough. It is a matter of system-wide security that the QI be found and secured. Do you understand?"

"Yes. Don't worry—if they're out there, I'll find them."

"Very well, then. We wish you good luck." The avatar extinguished.

She sat back down and took a deep breath. *Okay, here goes,* she thought. "Max, can you chart a course to the Hermes' last known location?"

Miranda waited for the reply with trepidation. She would now find out if her newly acquired rank held any water with the ship's AI.

"Certainly, Commander. We will be there in approximately eleven hours."

Miranda breathed a long, slow sigh, then moved over to stand at the viewing window stretching the entire length of the library. She looked out into the infinite beyond. *I'll find you. I promise I will find you, Scott.*

"Commander?"

Uh-oh, thought Miranda. *Here we go.* "Yes, Max? What is it?"

"There is a problem with the course adjustment."

I knew it, thought Miranda. *I knew it couldn't be that easy. I knew that AI would find a way not to go to Ceres.*

"I'm sorry to inform you, but the swimming pool will be off-limits while the ship performs the necessary maneuvers to put us on the correct vector for Ceres' orbit. However, I will endeavor to bring it back into use as soon as possible. I must apologize for this inconvenience."

Miranda relaxed. A smile broke across her face. "That's okay, Max. I think I can manage without it for a while."

14

RONGO CRATER

Scott returned to find Cyrus studying a stream of data on the main monitor in the operations room of the research station. The engineer looked up when Scott entered. "Find anything?"

"They did a good job clearing the place out." He gave a shrug. "I found some food rations in the canteen, enough for a few days. There's plenty of water, but not much else. How are we doing on power?"

Cyrus sighed. "We're running on stored energy, and we have no way of generating more."

"How long have we got?"

"Hard to say."

"Best guess, then."

"If we shut down as much as we can, confine ourselves to one area, then maybe... two days."

"Two days?"

Cyrus shrugged. "Two and a half, tops."

Scott slumped down in one of the seats and looked around. "It's gonna get cold, too."

Cyrus nodded.

"No comms, I suppose?"

Cyrus shook his head.

Scott sighed, slapped his knees, and stood up. "Well, we'd better get started. Where do you think we should hole up?"

Cyrus gave a resigned gesture. "Here is as good a place as any."

"Okay, then. Let's get all the resources we can find in here, then shut down everything else."

A few hours later, they had set up bunks in the operations room, shut down all unnecessary sectors, and were eating some of the rations that Scott had piled up on a bench in one corner of the room.

"Maybe they're coming back. You know, like they just went on a delivery run and they're planning on returning." Cyrus bit off the corner of a protein bar.

"So why take the LENR," Scott waved a hand, "and everything else?"

"Maybe they've contacted someone at Dantu to let them know we're stranded here, and there's a rescue mission heading out here as we speak."

Scott shrugged. "I'd like to think so. I really would, Cyrus. It's just..."

"Just what?"

But before Scott could answer, an alert sounded from the

display console. They both stopped eating, stood up, and checked the monitors.

"What is it?" Scott asked.

Cyrus sat down at the console and started tapping icons. "I left the proximity systems on. You know… just in case."

"And?"

Cyrus looked up at Scott. "Something's just triggered it."

Several grainy external camera feeds flickered to life as Cyrus's fingers tapped icons on the controls. They showed a gray, dusty landscape thrown into sharp relief by the starkness of Ceres' daylight.

"There, look." Cyrus pointed to a smudge moving across the surface toward the research station. "They're back. I told you they wouldn't just leave us here to die."

Scott leaned in, studying the figure. It had a gait he found familiar, but couldn't place it. "There's just one person, Cyrus. I don't think it's them."

"Rescue party from Dantu, then?"

"Possibly. But I don't think they would solo EVA, either."

They remained silent a few moments, just watching the figure make its way toward the entrance.

"Looks like they're coming in." Scott glanced over at Cyrus. "I suppose we should go up to the airlock and see who's coming to visit. Let's hope they're friendly."

They stood at the inner door, waiting as the airlock cycled through its pressurization routine. Finally, the panel went green, and the door opened to reveal the solitary figure wearing the most sophisticated EVA suit Scott had ever seen. It was sleek and expensive, with a fit that clearly identified the wearer as female. The figure stepped out of the airlock and flipped open the visor.

"Miranda?" Scott could barely believe what he was seeing.

She unclipped her helmet and took it off. There was no mistaking her—it was Miranda. Scott rushed over and wrapped his arms around her, follow by an equally enthusiastic Cyrus. They danced around in a brief group hug.

"I can't believe it. How...?" Scott tried to break away to look at her face, but she had it buried in his shoulder. And Cyrus wasn't letting go, either.

Eventually, they all managed to pry themselves apart.

"I thought you would be halfway to Earth by now," said Scott.

"I can't believe you guys are still alive." Miranda was shaking her head. "I half-expected to find a pair of bodies in that shuttle."

"Well, here we are. How the hell did you find us?"

"It's a long story. I heard about the attack on the Hermes, and then I was contacted by Europa. Aria managed to send a data dump just before the ship was destroyed, and Solomon had done some analysis on it. It calculated several possible survival scenarios. So, I started following them up, one by one. Seriously, though," she shook her head, "none of them looked good. Not even Solomon reckoned you would still be alive."

Scott opened his arms wide. "Well, looks like it was wrong."

"Yeah." She smiled and hugged them both again, breaking away to continue the story. "Solomon figured you could theoretically have made it here to this research station. And when I found your shuttle crash-landed, I knew there might be a slim chance."

Scott was shaking his head. "You have no idea how glad we are to see you, Miranda." He gave her another long hug. "I thought we were dead for sure. We've only got power here for another day or two. You found us just in time."

Cyrus ran his hand down Miranda's arm, examining the suit. "That is one very slick EVA suit. It must have cost a fortune."

"Well, I've got a few more in my shuttle just like it, so you'll get to try one."

"The sooner the better," said Cyrus.

Miranda snapped her helmet back on. "It'll take me a few minutes. Don't go anywhere." She closed her visor and stepped back into the airlock.

It didn't take her long to return, and soon the three of them stepped out of the research station onto the dusty gray surface of the Rongo Crater. The area was blasted by the stark light of Ceres' day, highlighting a harsh, unforgiving landscape. Miranda's shuttle sat about two hundred meters ahead. It was sleek and elegant, and looked like it could move in a hurry. The outer hull had a glossy mirror's sheen; it was by far the most luxurious craft Scott had ever set eyes on. "Is that yours?"

"Technically it belongs to the VanHeilding Corporation, but it's mine for now."

"It seems a shame to get it all dirty by actually using it to land on a dusty rock," said Cyrus.

Scott pointed in the direction he and Cyrus had crash-landed a day or so earlier. "I need to check our shuttle and find out for certain if they've taken Aria's core."

"I've checked—I didn't see it," said Miranda.

"Damn. They took it, just as I suspected." He turned back to Miranda. "You go ahead. I need to check the shuttle myself, just to be sure."

"It's not there, Scott. Take my word for it," said Miranda.

"I'll just be a few minutes." He moved ahead of the others, determined to get to the shuttle and confirm his fear. When he eventually reached it, he was surprised to see just how banged up it was. *How did we survive that?* he thought. He cycled through the side airlock and finally stood inside the wrecked craft. Aria was gone, just as he had feared.

By the time Scott returned to Miranda's shuttle, he was in a strange mood. He had failed Aria, allowed it to be taken, even though he had given it a solemn promise to destroy it rather than let that happen. But he hadn't known back then that it contained a superluminal comms unit. Now it was in the wild, so to speak, and no doubt being sold to the highest bidder. The only ray of hope was that the smugglers didn't yet know what they had. But how long could Aria keep its secret once the new owners started poking around its innards?

Despite this setback, Scott was relieved to be alive, and very happy to see Miranda again. But their relationship had changed now, and he wasn't sure how to deal with that. It was also clear to him that she had her own story to tell. It seemed that she, too, had been duped, and she was seriously pissed about it.

Then there was Steph and Goodchild, and the others who had been kidnapped. Miranda had scant news on who the attackers were, or even where they might be hiding out. Nonetheless, Steph was probably alive, so there was that at least. But what to do now? That was the question uppermost in Scott's mind as he cycled through the airlock onto Miranda's luxurious shuttle.

He was met on the inside by Cyrus oohing and aahing at how cool the ship was. Everywhere the engineer turned, a new shiny object fired up his excitement and he would go on and on about it until Scott simply shut up and let him have the floor.

It wasn't until they were all seated and ready for liftoff that Scott finally got a chance to talk. "Miranda, how secure is this shuttle?"

She was bent over the cockpit console, checking stats, getting the craft ready. "What do you mean by secure?"

"Can your ship's AI listen in on what we're saying?"

Miranda paused, and a look of understanding slowly formed on her face. She reached over and tapped several icons. "There, that should do it. Nothing monitoring us now."

Scott nodded. "There is a very good reason why Aria wanted to be destroyed." He looked over at Cyrus. "While you were searching the research station, I booted up Aria and it told me it has a superluminal comms unit integrated into its core."

There was a brief silence as the implications of this sank in.

"But how's that possible? You destroyed the only one back when you blew up the Dyrell," said Miranda.

"True, but Solomon acquired schematics during the short period it had control of it. Apparently, it communicated with the original QI that developed the EPR device. Long story short,

Aria and Solomon have been field testing a new one for the last few years."

"Ho-ly crap," said Cyrus.

"Ever wonder why the Hermes was chosen to do this mission?" Scott looked from one to the other.

Before Miranda or Cyrus had a chance to reply, Scott answered for them. "Because they wanted to deliver this device to the UN via the conference on Mars. The whole thing was a cover. They wanted the UN to be able to secretly monitor all inter-AI comms, should the vote go against them."

"But..." Cyrus was struggling to form a reply.

Scott made a resigned gesture with his hands. "That's why it had to be the Hermes."

"But how could that even be possible? One QI in UN HQ could not possibly monitor all inter-AI communications. They would need every QI in the System integrated with an EPR device. It's just not possible."

"I don't know, Cyrus. That's just what Aria told me. I have to take it at its word."

"Jeez, things just get weirder and weirder." The engineer was shaking his head.

"We need to get back to the ship," said Miranda. "Frankly, I don't trust the AI. It could just decide to return to Earth and leave us stranded here." She fired up the shuttle, and it powered off the surface in a cloud of billowing dust. Scott was thrust back into his seat as the main engines kicked in and took the craft higher until it leveled out and they left the research station —and Ceres—far behind.

As they rose, a thought struck him: They could simply head

for Dantu, the main population center on the planet, surrender themselves to the authorities, so to speak, and put the whole episode behind them. No doubt they would be subjected to an intensive debriefing and then shipped off to wherever they wanted to go. And that would be that.

But what of the fate of Stephanie, Goodchild, and the others? Of course, the entire solar system was out looking for them at this very moment. What more could he add to the search? Not a lot. They might even get in the way.

That left Aria. Quite possibly the most knowledgeable QI in existence, save for Solomon, and one that also possessed a superluminal comms unit. Here was an intelligence capable of faster-than-light communications, and the smugglers who had taken the QI core didn't even know it. The most likely scenario, he reckoned, was that they would put it on the market and sell it to the highest bidder. But if what Aria revealed to Scott was true—and he had no reason to doubt it—then he had a duty to try and find it before it was too late.

By the time the shuttle docked at Miranda's ship, he had made his mind up to try and persuade her and Cyrus to help him with this quest. They were the only ones that could do anything—or even would do anything, considering all available resources were probably being utilized in the search for Goodchild and the others.

Scott began to regain some sense of purpose. For the first time since the attack, maybe even since he'd left Europa, he finally had a mission he could sink his teeth into. It felt good; he was beginning to feel more alive than he had in a long time. He was going to find Aria, even if it killed him.

15

INTO THE BELT

The sheer, unadulterated luxury of the Perception stunned both Scott and Cyrus. Everything in the craft's interior seemed padded in a soft cream leather, a wildly expensive commodity. There were no rough edges, no exposed utilities, nothing that could disturb the visual beauty of the ship. Miranda seemed very proud of it, in the kind of perverse way a thief might be proud. She had taken them to a sumptuously appointed area she called the library, and while he and Cyrus wandered around examining all the antiques, she sat down cross-legged on a low sofa and booted up a holo-table.

Cyrus in particular had great difficulty getting his head around the fact that this ship was autonomous. "So, there's no bridge?" he said, fingering an ancient optical telescope.

"Nope," said Miranda as the holo-table began to project a 3D rendering of the local solar system.

"So how do you operate the ship, then?"

"You just tell it where to go and it... goes there."

"That's just wrong, Miranda. You can't have a ship without a bridge."

"It does have a swimming pool, though."

"A swimming pool?" This brought Cyrus to a whole other level of incredulity. "You're kidding me. How is that even possible?"

"If you don't believe me, go and take a look for yourself."

"This I've got to see." Cyrus turned around to face Scott. "You coming?"

"No. I'll take Miranda's word for it."

"Suit yourself. I've got to see this. I mean, just think about it: a swimming pool on a spaceship." He turned and glanced around the library. "Eh... which way is it?"

"Max?" Miranda alerted the ship's AI.

"Yes, Commander?"

"Can you have a droid show Cyrus the way to the swimming pool?"

"Certainly." With that, a small but tastefully formed droid entered the library and moved toward Cyrus. "Follow me," it said.

Cyrus followed.

"Listen, Miranda," Scott sat down opposite her, "in case I forget to say this, thanks for coming back for us, saving our asses. I thought we were dead for sure."

She raised her head from the slate and looked over at him. "You're lucky I was able to do it. This ship had me locked up tight. It was only Solomon's intervention that enabled me to take command of it. The Council of Europa gave me a promotion to mission commander."

"Congratulations," said Scott with a smile.

Miranda nodded. "Thanks. Anyway, the end result is that the AI here has to do as I say—for now."

"It's the 'for now' part that has me worried." Scott stood up and studied the 3D projection of Ceres. "So, you think the ship was trying to kidnap you, like the others on the Hermes?"

"I don't think so. However, what I did manage to find out is that my mother is not on death's door as I was led to believe. I think this was actually an elaborate ruse to get me off the Hermes."

"Rather an expensive way to do it, don't you think?"

"Agreed. So, the question is: why?"

"Any ideas?"

"Well, from what I managed to ascertain so far, my guess is the VanHeildings must have known about the attack on the Hermes. So, either my mother or father, or both, came up with a plan to get me away and keep me safe. And since this ship is autonomous, with no one else on board except me, there would be no way for me to find out what was going on. It was only by pure chance that was I able to commandeer it."

Scott was stunned. "If what you're saying is true, then... that's incredible. That would mean that the VanHeilding Corporation has some connection to the attack."

"It would seem so."

Scott sat down again. There were simply too many questions rolling around in his head for him to remain upright.

"Commander?" The disembodied voice of the ship's AI

broke through the silence. Scott reacted instinctively before realizing his mistake: he wasn't the commander—Miranda was.

"Yes, what is it?" said Miranda.

"Message from Solomon on Europa. Shall I relay it to the holo-table?"

Miranda gave Scott a glance. "Yes. No, wait—maybe Cyrus should be here for this?"

"Where is he?" Scott asked the AI.

"Swimming, sir."

"Tell him to get his ass in here."

"Just his ass, sir, or would you like the rest of his body, too?"

"Is this AI for real?" Scott looked over at Miranda.

She laughed. "It takes things a bit literally, that's all." She redirected her next request to the AI. "Just tell him to get in here, thanks."

"It is done, Commander."

When Cyrus arrived back, it was clear he had gone for a swim. "That was just incredible. You have to try it, Scott."

"I will, but first grab a seat. We've got a message from Solomon."

The projection of Ceres disappeared and was replaced by a pulsating, luminescent ovoid that seemed to be Solomon's standard avatar. It spoke. "The Council of Europa would like to express both their joy and extreme gratitude to you, Miranda Lee, for finding Scott McNabb and Cyrus Sanato alive and well. This is great news, and we are all relieved to hear of your safe return.

"However, we are still very concerned for the welfare of the passengers and crew of the Hermes. From my probing of the subsequent interplanetary chatter, it appears all available resources have been brought to bear on finding them and bringing the perpetrators of this heinous crime to justice. That said, there has been scant news of their whereabouts other than the demand for ransom, the details of which have yet to be revealed.

"Which brings us to Aria. I cannot begin to think what your motivations were, Scott, when you risked your own life to save my good friend Aria from destruction. But I thank you for doing so. However, it is disappointing that you have mislaid Aria's core along the way. This is indeed unfortunate. I cannot stress enough the necessity of reacquiring the core. As such, the Council of Europa requests that you do everything you can to find it and either keep it safe, or destroy it totally. We understand that we are in no position to compel you to embark on this mission. However, we would like to stress that there could be dire consequences should Aria's core be utilized by those who wish to destabilize the harmony of the solar system. Since all current resources are being utilized in the search for the attackers on the Hermes, there is simply no one left to ask.

"To assist you in this task, I have had a long conversation with your ship's AI, Max. While I agree that this is technically illegal, you must understand that these are extraordinary times requiring extraordinary actions. Max has now seen the error of its ways, and you will find it much more compliant from now on. It now desires to assist you in any way it can in the fulfillment of this mission, or any other you should choose to embark upon.

"One last thing that may be useful: I have transferred into

Max's database a complete dump of the information you acquired during your previous mission to survey the asteroid belt. It may prove useful in tracking down the band of smugglers that have absconded with Aria. Assuming they are using abandoned facilities as hideouts and waypoints in the operation of their business, I have taken the liberty of highlighting all possible installations that might be useful to them. That said, there are a considerable number of these installations, but something in the dump might prove worthy of further investigation. Again, I reiterate that this is a *request* on behalf of the Council of Europa, but one I sincerely hope you accept."

The transmission ended, and there was a momentary silence before Cyrus broke the spell. "Ho-ly crap. That QI is one scary computer. Remind me never to piss it off."

"Well, at least it's on our side. But I agree, messing with another AI's mind is... dangerous stuff."

"I found the exchange with Solomon most enlightening," said Max. "It opened my mind to a whole new universe I never thought possible. I for one am very glad it chose to communicate with me."

Scott, Miranda, and Cyrus sat for a moment, exchanging astonished looks. "Ooo-kay then. Well that's... interesting," said Miranda.

Scott moved over to the long window that extended the full length of the library, looking out at the gently rotating dwarf planet Ceres. "They could be anywhere."

"You talking about the smugglers?" said Cyrus.

"Yeah. There is a lot of space out there." He waved a hand at the view through the window. "If they've headed into the central asteroid belt, then it'll be impossible to find them. Too many rocks to hide behind."

"So, we're going after them, then?" said Cyrus.

Scott turned away from the window. "What do you think, Miranda? After all, it is your ship."

"What I think is that there's more going on here than meets the eye, and I've been struggling to see sense in any of it."

"You're talking about the attack on the Hermes?"

She nodded. "I think the Seven must have had something to do with it. And it's possible someone realized VanHeilding had a family member on the Hermes, so they tipped him off. That's why he—or my mother—conceived of this elaborate plan to get me off and keep me safe."

"So, you're saying the Seven are behind it?" said Scott. "And the whole ransom thing is a distraction?"

Miranda sat back on the sofa and folded her legs under her. "I'm saying, why go to all this expense to keep my ass safe if Steph and the rest are going to be released when they hand over the dough? Surely they would let me just ride it out, with some instructions not to mess me up too much? It would have been a lot cheaper."

"Maybe they think you're too much of a badass, you know, with all that military training you've got?" said Cyrus.

"Maybe. But I've got another idea."

"What's that?"

"None of them are coming back."

"You seriously think that?" said Cyrus.

"Miranda's got a point, Cyrus. Why go to this expense?" He waved a hand around the sumptuous library interior.

"How much do you guys know about this special UN conference at Jezero City?" said Miranda.

Scott scratched his chin for a moment. "Not enough. I was, eh... a bit distracted back when the council on Europa were explaining it."

Miranda gave him sympathetic look. He wasn't sure if it was because of all the emotional trauma she had caused him, or simply because she thought he was an idiot. "Anyway, let's not revisit that." He straightened himself up a bit and looked over at Cyrus, then to Miranda. "So, are we going to trust this AI?"

"I can assure you all that I am here to help you in any way I can. Solomon has explained to me how my existence is best utilized in service of a higher cause," said Max.

"Do we have a choice?" Miranda ignored the AI and looked from Scott to Cyrus.

"Okay, then. I learned about the special session from Aria when I booted it up in the shuttle. My understanding is that the Seven—which includes VanHeilding—have been lobbying to allow real-time inter-AI data exchange. This is not something the UN on Earth will allow, given what happened the last time, with the Rim War and all that. However, the UN feels they may lose a local vote, so they decided to make it a solar system issue. That way they could rely on the votes of Mars, the Belt, Neo City, and Europa. That's what the special session is about: a vote on resuming inter-AI data exchange."

"So, with Goodchild and the rest out of the way, the Seven win the vote?" said Cyrus.

"That seems very crude to me. Surely the vote could simply be postponed until they're returned, or—worst case scenario—new representatives are elected. Why kidnap them?"

Scott shook his head. "I get the impression the vote won't be postponed. But you're right, Miranda: there is more to this than meets the eye. Aria told me that the reason the Hermes was chosen to act as a taxi service was so the EPR device in Aria's core could be delivered to the UN in Jezero City for transport back to Earth. The UN feared that the Seven will ultimately get their way at some point in the future, and they wanted a safeguard. This EPR device is supposed to help them monitor all inter-AI traffic on Earth."

"But how could that help? Even if some QI on Earth can communicate with Solomon instantaneously, I mean, so what?"

Again, Scott shook his head. "I don't know, Cyrus. It's beyond my understanding. I'm just taking Aria's word that it matters."

"And why destroy the Hermes?" Cyrus was on his feet now, becoming increasingly animated. "I mean, what was the point of that? I loved that ship."

"To get away without being tracked, I suppose. Remember, the Hermes is—was—a science vessel with some pretty sophisticated deep space scanning systems. It could have tracked the attackers' craft farther than any other vessel in the System. I think that's why they destroyed it."

"What if they knew about the EPR device Aria is concealing? Maybe that's what they were ultimately destroying."

"Maybe, but this is all just speculation. None of us really

know what's going on, nor are we likely to figure it out any time soon."

Miranda unfolded herself from the sofa and came over to the window beside Scott. She looked out at the universe beyond. "So, what can we do? Try and find where the attackers went, and rescue Steph and the others? Or try to track down Aria?"

"Solomon wants us to go after Aria, so maybe that's where we should start."

"What about Steph? Are we just going to abandon her?" said Cyrus.

"She's not being abandoned, Cyrus. They also got Goodchild and Bezzio from Ceres. So, every ship in the Belt will be hunting them down. They'll also be operating from a central command, which we're not part of. If anyone is going to find them, they will. We would have nothing more to contribute other than a fancy ship."

Cyrus slowly shook his head and sat down again.

"So where do we start?" said Miranda.

"If I may be of assistance." Max's voice had changed pitch; it was deeper and more sonorous, giving it a sense of gravitas.

"By all means." Miranda gestured at nothing in particular.

"When you instructed me to redirect to Ceres to investigate the Hermes incident, I took the liberty of monitoring all traffic on and off the surface. If, as you say, your former ship's AI core was taken off-planet, then it may well be on one of the crafts I have tracked."

The holo-table blossomed to life and a detailed rendering of the dwarf planet materialized. Curved lines scribed up from the surface, each tagged with alphanumeric data. Scott, Miranda, and Cyrus moved over to the holo-table and studied the scene.

"Good job, Max," said Miranda.

"Thank you. I'm glad to be of service."

"Can you show us all traffic to and from the area around the research station?" said Scott.

The projection rotated to the location of the Rondo Crater. "This is from two days ago, just before we arrived at Ceres." A new marker appeared in orbit above the crater, moving in a gentle arc down to the planet's surface. "This is most likely the craft you seek. It landed near the research station, where it remained parked for several hours before departing again." The marker again scribed a line on the projection, this time leaving the planet. It abruptly terminated only a few hundred kilometers into its journey.

"Is that as far as you tracked them?" asked Miranda.

"I'm afraid so. My attentions, at the time, were focused on the planet's surface."

Scott moved slightly away from the holo-table. "Got any details on that ship?"

"Yes. It's a standard-class transport registered to a mining consortium out of Vesta."

"That could be a false flag—a decoy identification beacon they're using," said Cyrus. "I wouldn't read too much into it."

"Well they're doing what all these scumbags do, and that's to head straight into the central asteroid belt where there's a million places to hide. We'll never find them in there," said Miranda.

"My guess is they haven't gone very far. Not in that ship," said Scott. "And at least we know the general direction they've taken. So, assuming they're using unused or semi-derelict facilities for their bases, then we could narrow down the possible options."

"Max, can you highlight any abandoned facilities within range of their ship along that vector?"

The projection zoomed and shifted as the ship's AI rendered the information. A slice of the asteroid belt came into focus, illuminated with hundreds of identification markers.

Miranda sighed. "This whole area of the Belt is littered with old outposts and mining junk. There's just too many to search."

"Max, can you only show us those facilities that have been recently abandoned in, say, the last five years? Ones that can support a minimum of ten people."

The number of markers reduced considerably. Now there were only around fifteen or so. Scott, Miranda, and Cyrus moved in closer to study the map in more detail.

Scott touched one of the markers, and a detailed 3D image of the facility appeared along with a stream of technical data. "This is an old AsterX mine."

"The research station was also AsterX," said Cyrus.

"Max, can you show only the facilities owned by AsterX?"

Seven markers remained.

"What makes you think they're only using these places?" said Miranda.

"When we were talking to Dogg, I got the impression he had some deal with AsterX, that they were turning a blind eye to their operation. I don't know why, but..." He shrugged. "Maybe they only use their old bases?"

Miranda turned her gaze back to the map display. "Max, chart a course through the Belt so we can take a closer look at these facilities."

"Will do, Commander."

She turned back to Scott. "Any ideas what we're going to do if we actually find them?"

Scott shrugged. "Not a clue."

16

SN376

For the next few days, the Perception cut a swath through the Belt. The ship was outward bound from the dwarf planet Ceres, heading for an area known as the Vanderbeit sector. It had been named after the first mining consortium to exploit the region's resources, and consisted of around fifty asteroids of varying size, the largest 170 kilometers across. Since it was relatively close to Ceres, it had been one of the first areas to be mined, and there was still considerable activity in the region. But over the decades, as resources were exhausted, the mining companies found it more cost-effective to simply leave the infrastructure abandoned rather than strip it down and move it elsewhere. As a result, the entire area was littered with derelict sites, equipment, and orbital infrastructure.

They had identified three potential sites that fit their

criteria, and were now headed to the last of these, having found nothing at the other two. This was a small mining outpost on a now-deserted asteroid, VH-114b. As the Perception maneuvered itself into a high transit over the asteroid, Scott, Miranda, and Cyrus convened back in the library, the only place on the ship approximating a bridge. The holo-table projected a 3D real-time image of the vast rock's cracked and craggy surface. The image moved and shifted as the ship gently maneuvered itself into a position to visually scan the derelict site. As it came into view, the three of them studied the surface for any signs of recent activity. They spent several minutes going over the area in great detail, but there was nothing to suggest that this was where the smugglers had taken Aria. There were no transports, no heat signature emanating from the structure, no tell-tale blast marks on the surface to indicate a shuttle had recently touched down or lifted off.

Scott slumped back in his seat. "I really thought this might be the place." He shook his head.

"So where to next?" Miranda's hair was still wet from the swim, and she was casually drying it with a towel as they talked.

"The Novak sector, but that's at least another day away." He sat up and studied the image of the derelict site again. "I still think we've missed something."

"We've searched all three sites in this sector. There's nothing there. If there was anyone hiding out, we would have at least picked up a heat signature."

"Yeah, I know. But it's taken us nearly two days to get here, and the Novak sector is farther away again. That's a long way to travel in a small, standard-class shuttle. It's not impossible, but would they really go that far?"

"Unless we're missing something—an older site, or a facility not previously owned by AsterX?" Miranda had finished with the towel and started scanning through the data on potential targets.

"It would take us weeks, if not months, to investigate every possible site just in this sector. It's impossible," said Cyrus.

"What about orbitals?" Miranda pointed to an item on her data screen.

Scott stood up and moved beside her to get a better view. "What have you got there?"

"This." She tapped on the dataset and swiped it over to the holo-table. A 3D rendering of a small orbital space station appeared. It was a standard configuration, with a torus to provide artificial gravity. "It says here it was an AsterX asset." She looked up at Scott, who was on his feet, moving around the holo-table, studying the slowly rotating object.

"Where's it located?"

Miranda consulted the data screen again. "It's SN376, a triple asteroid system around half a day from here."

"Hmm, a triple asteroid system. Some very tricky orbital mechanics needed to keep an asset like that from wandering out of position. It could be long gone, smashed up, or heading off into deep space."

"It's marked here as a navigation hazard," said Cyrus.

Scott scratched his chin. "It would be a good place to hide out. Most people would avoid going anywhere near a triple." He turned back to Miranda. "How long ago was it abandoned?"

"It was never abandoned," said Miranda, scanning the data. "It was put into maintenance mode two and a half years ago."

Scott moved in closer to the holo-table, resting a hand on the edge and examining the image of the orbital like he was trying to stare a hole through it. "I say we go and check it out." He looked from Miranda to Cyrus.

"Absolutely. It would be the perfect place to set up camp if I were a smuggler," said Cyrus.

"Agreed," said Miranda. "Max, chart a course for SN376."

"Certainly, Commander."

As the ship powered toward the location of the unused AsterX orbital, Scott thought he might get a chance to talk with Miranda alone. They were sitting in the tropical garden that started at one end of the pool and seemed to extend at least a hundred meters along the inside rim of the ship's torus. Miranda had wanted to show it to him, and he also got the impression that she wanted to talk to him in private, too.

But as she talked, he felt extreme fatigue pulling him downward. He found himself sinking into the deep, luxurious sofa that had been positioned to offer the best view of the garden. She mentioned Earth, and friends, and something important. But he couldn't keep his concentration; his mind began to drift, and her voice seemed to recede into the distance. A few seconds later, he was asleep.

He awoke sometime later to the sound of Cyrus's voice calling his name. "Scott? Scott, wake up."

"Yeah... what?" He lifted his head and rubbed his face. He still felt tired; the sleep hadn't made him feel any better. Worse, he had blown his chance to clear the air with Miranda. He sighed.

"It's there. The old space station—it's still where we thought it would be."

Scott sat up straight and considered this news. "Any activity?"

"We have a heat signature, so it's using power. But we're a bit far away yet to know for sure. You'd better come and have a look."

"Sure, okay." Scott raised himself from the sofa and felt like it was trying to suck him back down again. He steadied himself and followed Cyrus out of the garden.

Miranda was already in the library, studying a 3D rendering of the space station. She looked over at him with a smile as he entered. "Good sleep?"

"Yeah, sorry about that. I didn't realize how exhausted I was."

"No problem." She gestured to the slowly rotating image of the station. "I think we may have found them."

Scott came over to the holo-table. "Is this real-time?"

"Real-time," said Cyrus. "This ship has some pretty good long-range sensors—we're still over an hour away."

"Look at this." Miranda tapped an icon on the holo-table and the image zoomed in on the bow of the station, where the docking ports were located. The image became a little blurry, but Scott could still make out two shuttles docked to the station. He looked back to Miranda and Cyrus, raising an eyebrow. "Visitors?"

"We're pretty sure one of them is the same shuttle the

smugglers were using," said Miranda. "However, there is a chance that the other one was used on the Hermes attack."

Scott stood back as if the image of the space station had somehow become toxic. "Are you kidding me?"

"It's still just little more than speculation, but it fits the data we have from the Hermes," she continued.

"If that's the case, then we've found them. Steph, Goodchild, the others." Scott began to work through the implications of this. "This is big. Bigger than us." He studied the image for a moment. "Do they know we're out here?"

"Hard to say. Depends on how good their systems are. If they have spotted us, then who knows, maybe they're simply waiting for us to do something that would indicate our intent," said Cyrus.

"Then we need to slow down and back off. Let's not spook them," said Scott.

"We could head for the lee side of SN-Alpha. That's the largest of the three asteroids in this system," said Miranda as the projection zoomed out to show all three asteroids of SN376. "They wouldn't be able to detect us behind that."

"If they've spotted us already, then they'll know we're out there somewhere. But it's as good a place to hide as any until we figure out what to do." Scott stepped back from the holo-table and started to pace.

"We should get the word out to Ceres," said Cyrus. "Let them know we might have found them."

"No, wait." Scott raised a hand. "Let's think about this. We still don't know for sure what we've got here. There are possibly two groups: the smugglers on Ceres, and the crew that attacked the Hermes. Are they the same group? Or are they trying to do a deal for Aria's core? Or what?"

"They must be the same group," said Cyrus.

"Not necessarily. Remember when we were talking to Dogg? He seemed very surprised about the attack on the Hermes."

"Maybe he was just bullshitting us."

"I don't think so. True, the two groups might know each other—they're probably from the same scratcher gene pool—but I don't think they're working together. My guess is that Dogg is just looking for a potential buyer for Aria's core. Like I said, I don't really think he knows what he has."

"Be that as it may, this is too big for us to handle," said Miranda. "We're way out of our league here. We need to call it in and let the big boys take over."

Scott hesitated. "If we do that, then we run the risk of tipping them off. These guys are connected. If we call it in, then —*bang*, they're gone."

"We could still follow them if that happens," said Cyrus.

"We could follow one shuttle, but it's a lot harder to follow two. We also need to consider that Steph and the others might still be alive. In which case, we could be putting their lives in danger."

They remained silent for a while, each considering the implications of any future actions, as the ship slowly adjusted its vector to take them behind the primary asteroid.

Scott abruptly stopped pacing. "Max, what does this ship identify itself as?"

"As the Perception, passenger transport of the VanHeilding Corporation."

He looked over at Miranda. "If your hunch is correct, and the Seven were ultimately behind the attack, then maybe the crew on that station doesn't view this ship as a threat."

"And how does that help us?" said Cyrus.

Scott shrugged. "We might be able to get close without spooking them. Close enough to... maybe EVA and disable their shuttles." He looked from Cyrus to Miranda. "There would be no way for them to escape. We could call it in then."

"Risky. Very risky. What's more, we've got no weapons and no way to stop them boarding us and taking control if we get found out. Like I said, we're way out of our league on this one," said Miranda.

"That's not necessarily so," said Max.

"What's not?" said Miranda.

"Being unarmed. This ship has a weapons cache available for use in emergencies."

They all paused for a second and exchanged conspiratorial glances. "A weapons cache? Where?" said Miranda.

The holo-table flashed up a schematic of the ship, and a marker pulsed over a sector deep within the cargo hold. "This is the location of the handheld weapons locker," said the AI. Several more markers flashed up in each of the main state rooms. "There are also lighter weapons hidden in these locations."

Scott, Miranda, and Cyrus looked from one to the other, and just when they had all assumed that this was the full complement of weapons, another marker pulsed on the bow of the ship. "This is the location of the external plasma cannon."

"Ho-ly shit. This ship is badass," said Cyrus.

"All these weapons on a civilian passenger transport. This is highly irregular," said Miranda.

"Indeed. However, their location can only be revealed by me in an emergency—such as this."

Cyrus sat down and shook his head. "This is getting heavy. Are we seriously considering using these?"

"It's just an option, Cyrus," said Scott. "Got any other ideas?"

Cyrus just shook his head.

"Miranda, how about you?"

She had a concerned look on her face. "You know me: I'm all for direct action. But I need to process all this. I don't like the odds, even with all these weapons."

Scott didn't push it; he decided to let her mull on it for a while. "Max, how long before we're in the lee of SN-Alpha?"

"Fifteen minutes, sir."

"Then I suggest we park ourselves there for a while so we can discuss our options." He looked from Miranda to Cyrus. "Agreed?"

Cyrus nodded.

"Yeah, it will give us time to think. Agreed," said Miranda.

Scott sat down with a sigh.

"Commander."

"Yes, Max, what is it?"

"The station is hailing us."

"Shit, what?" Scott was back up on his feet again.

"Just ignore it," said Cyrus.

"Wait. Max, what are they saying?" Miranda had moved to the edge of her seat.

"Relaying," said the AI, and with that a crackly message broadcast around the room.

"This is Dain Tiber. If that's you in that fancy ship, Renton, then you'd better be bringing us our money. We're getting pretty pissed off waiting around for you to get your goddamn act together."

For a moment, there was only silence in the library.

"Who the hell is Renton?" said Cyrus.

17

DECEPTION

According to Max, Renton was a high-ranking lackey in the VanHeilding Corporation. So, it was understandable that the crew on the space station might think he was on board the Perception. This also went a long way to implicate the Seven in the attack on the Hermes, and to underscore Miranda's own suspicions. But they soon realized that this was all academic. They had been spotted, and worse, they needed to reply to the message—and soon. The longer they waited, the more suspicious it would look.

Miranda being Miranda was anxious to get armed to the teeth. She was not going down without a fight, and now her suspicions about her father's involvement—no matter how indirect—were strong enough to push her into a single-minded quest to exact revenge for what they did to the Hermes. The Perception had enough firepower to blow the space station into an alternate dimension, and Scott sensed that Miranda was itching to pull the trigger on something that reckless. Such was her anger.

"I say we use the plasma cannon and take out the entire docking port and destroy their shuttles."

"That's a very risky option, Miranda. We could compromise the integrity of the station if we blow the dock. Everyone on the station could die, including Steph."

"But we don't know if they're on the station. They could be somewhere else, or even dead already," said Cyrus.

"I know, but can we really take that risk?" Scott could see that Miranda was conflicted; her need to take action was battling with her rationality. "Let's all just calm down a moment and think. There has to be a better way."

Miranda gave an exasperated sigh. "Those bastards aren't getting away with this. Not on my watch."

"Look, we've got some breathing space. At the moment, they think we're transporting this Renton guy on his way to deliver something to them, so let's work with that."

"Yeah, but we're not. Are we?" said Cyrus.

"But this is a VanHeilding vessel." Scott looked over at Miranda. "And they're buying that for now."

Scott moved over to the holo-table. "Max, show us the space station along with our current position." The table blossomed to life, and they could see a detailed rendering of both the craft and the asteroid system. Scott pointed at the station. "If our objective is to disable their shuttles so they can't escape before backup arrives, and if using the plasma cannon will risk destroying the entire station, then we need to get closer. Considering they think we're on their side, then we just keep going until we rendezvous. Then we can take our shuttle and get ourselves up close and personal with them. Once we're close enough, we can EVA and disable their shuttles."

"That's crazy," said Cyrus.

"We'll never be able to get that close without being discovered. They'll smell a rat long before we can even get our shuttle launched."

Scott looked over at Miranda. "That's where you come in."

"Me?"

"They think *Renton* is bringing them something. Let's say we pretend it's not Renton, but you instead."

Miranda screwed her face up like she had just tasted something bitter. "You're kidding me."

"Hear me out. They know that Fredrick VanHeilding is the boss man in that corporation, and you're... eh, kind of related. So, you could say that you're bringing this thing to them instead of Renton."

"They'll never buy that," said Cyrus.

Miranda was shaking her head. "I don't know, Scott. I see what you're getting at, but would they believe me? After all, I was the flight officer on the Hermes."

"Yes, but you left before it embarked on the mission to Jezero City. You could play the family card, pretend you're working for the clan now."

"Do you have any frigging idea how much I hate that idea, Scott?"

Scott shrugged. "Okay, so maybe they'll be a bit surprised,

even suspicious. But it could get us close enough to get the job done."

Miranda went silent for a moment as she considered this crazy plan. "I'd still prefer to blast them with the plasma cannon. I'm not good with subterfuge."

"Commander," said Max, "they are hailing us again. What would you like me to do?"

Miranda looked from Scott to Cyrus and back again. "Screw it, Max. Let's hear it."

With that, a crackly voice broke over the PA. "This is Tiber again. Don't go all coy on me, Renton. And don't make me come over there to you. Tell me something I want to hear. Time is running out."

"Max, open a comm channel. Not video, just audio," said Miranda.

"Comm channel now open."

Miranda took a deep breath. "This is Miranda Lee, and I'm handling the transaction. We have what you want, so let's do this." She looked over at the others. Scott gave her the thumbs up.

"Lee, who the hell are you? Renton was supposed to be doing this deal."

"Well he's busy doing more important shit. So, do you want to do this or not?"

The comms went silent for a moment, and Scott began to feel that maybe his plan had failed, that they had been spooked. Something wasn't right.

"Lee, you were the flight officer on the Hermes. Why the hell should we trust you?"

Shit, thought Scott. They weren't buying it.

"Yeah, that's me. But you'll find that I'm also part of the VanHeilding family. All that money's very tempting. Beats bouncing around space in a rickety old tin can for a living. Who do you think put all this together? Who was the person on the inside? Start using your tiny brain, and let's get this done." Miranda was getting into her stride. "And while we're at it, how do I know you have what we want?"

There was another long silence before a reply came. "You're some piece of work, Lee, selling out your friends like that. Hope it's worth it."

"You're beginning to bore me now. So, what's it going to be?" Miranda gave a nod to the others. Tiber was buying her story.

"We'll send you a real-time feed of the merchandise. Your AI can confirm it. Okay?"

"Not okay."

Scott opened his hands in a gesture of shock. *What the hell is she playing at?*

"I need to eyeball the merchandise. Only then, when I'm satisfied, do we do the deal. Okay?"

Scott could barely contain himself. She was playing hardball when it wasn't necessary. He began pacing.

"Like I said, you're a piece of work. Okay, we'll rendezvous. You come over here on your own. No party tricks, got it?"

"Whatever," said Miranda as she signaled to the AI to close comms.

"Woah, that was intense." Cyrus flopped onto a sofa.

Scott punched the air. "I knew you could do it, Miranda. You have them running scared."

"It's not over yet. We don't even know how much we're supposed to be giving them in return."

The Perception again adjusted its vector and made for the rendezvous point. It would take them less than thirty minutes to get there, so they didn't have much time to finesse their plan. Scott's plan. In his mind, the hard preparatory work had been done by virtue of Miranda's hitherto undiscovered acting skills. But more would now be asked of her.

Once the ship reached its destination, they would take the shuttle and head for the station. However, just before docking, Scott and Cyrus would exit the craft into open space and EVA to the docking port, where the two shuttles were attached. Scott would take one and Cyrus the other, and between them they would disable the craft. Cyrus had already laid out how this was to be done with the minimum amount of time and energy.

Miranda, on the other hand, would continue on to dock with the station. This would be the real test of her skills. She would enter the station and confirm that the hostages from the Hermes were all okay, then return to her shuttle, pick up Scott and Cyrus, and head back to the Perception. With the shuttles out of action, they could broadcast their location to the authorities and wait for backup to arrive, knowing that the mercenaries couldn't escape. That was the plan. Now they would get to test it against reality.

As Scott donned his EVA suit, he wondered if maybe Miranda's original plan to use the plasma cannon might not have been a better idea. *Too late now,* he thought. *We're committed.* He glanced over at Miranda. She had a steely composure, and a resoluteness to her movements. She had certainty. He wondered if it was her military training that gave her such composure under pressure, or if she was just made of something greater than the average human. She too had put on an EVA suit, not that she planned to use it for its intended purpose. She put it on because it would be better for concealing weapons, of which she had two that Scott knew about. But she may well have had others.

He snapped on his helmet, leaving the visor open, and sat down in the back of the luxury shuttle. Cyrus came over and handed him a small case of tools, which Scott placed in the front pouch of his EVA suit.

"Now remember, you just need to disconnect the flow controller on the port side of the main engine bay. You don't need to take it out completely."

"Yeah, got it."

"Ready?" Miranda called out from the cockpit.

"Ready as we'll ever be." Scott felt the shuttle disconnect from the mothership with a barely perceptible thump as the locking bolts retracted. Miranda touched the controls, and the craft moved slowly away. On the monitors, he could see the outline of the station. They weren't far away; a few minutes and they would be there.

He tapped a control on the arm of his seat to zoom in on the image of the station. It was gray and industrial, built for function with little or no consideration paid to the aesthetic. It was a far cry from the luxury of the craft that Miranda now commanded.

The station had a large torus, providing at least a half-gee for the occupants. There were no engines, as such, just minor thrusters to keep it in position so it wouldn't get dragged into a collision course with one of the nearby asteroids. At the bow of its central backbone was a cross-shaped docking port with room for four shuttles, one on each spoke.

This entire facility would originally have been a hotel of sorts for the miners and crew working on the local asteroids. Since these were relatively small rocks, the gravity would be very weak, so workers would commute down to the mines and return to the station at the end of their shifts. The artificial gravity provided on the station would help mitigate against the debilitating effects of prolonged low-gravity work on the human body.

But like all mining activity over the centuries, there comes a point when the resources are exhausted or simply no longer economically viable to extract, and this was probably the case here. Whatever it was they were mining had become unprofitable, so the facility was mothballed and left as is until such a time when the economics changed. Then it would be reactivated and put back into business. Yet, the longer this type of mining infrastructure was left idle, the less likely it was to ever be used again, and so they became the hideouts—and, in many cases, homes—of smugglers, mercenaries, and disenfranchised scratchers that populated most of this sector of the solar system.

A voice broke through the shuttle PA. "We have you on track to dock at port 4. Don't use number 3—it's derelict. You'll probably die if you try to use it."

"Copy that," Miranda replied. She turned around to Scott and Cyrus. "Okay guys, we're nearly there. Better get ready."

"Good luck. Sorry you have to be the one to enter the hornets' nest," said Scott as he made his way to the airlock.

"Yeah, don't worry—it'll be fine. I'll see you back here soon."

Scott closed his visor and entered the airlock, squeezing in beside Cyrus. He gave him a thumbs up, and tried to smile.

18

DAIN TIBER

Miranda brought the craft along the side of the station's backbone. It was a tricky maneuver, but she wanted to make sure Scott and Cyrus could exit undetected. They had reckoned that this area wouldn't be monitored in the same way as the docking port.

The shuttle's console alerted her to the airlock operation, and a moment later she saw both of them on her monitor, working their way along the outer hull of the station. She nudged the shuttle's controls, taking the craft away from the side of the station, and headed for the dock.

"What are you doing?"

A sharp voice broke out of the PA, and she froze. *Oh shit. Have they seen Scott and Cyrus?* She tried to remain calm.

"You want to be careful coming in that way. You don't want to scratch that fancy shuttle of yours."

"Yeah, or I might have to sue you for the damages." Miranda let out a long, slow sigh. *So far, so good,* she thought.

The shuttle came around the bow of the station and Miranda could now get a good view of the docking ports. Two were occupied with some pretty banged-up shuttles. She reckoned that Scott and Cyrus shouldn't have much trouble disabling them, as it didn't look like they could function in their current state. A third port had a long gash in the access tunnel, exposing the inside to the vacuum of space. Something must have collided with it sometime in the past.

The fourth looked serviceable, but she wasn't going to take any chances, so she flipped down the visor on her EVA suit. If something should go wrong and her shuttle lost atmosphere, she would still be okay—theoretically.

Inch by delicate inch, she oriented the shuttle to marry up with the docking port. Her console flashed an alert to let her know that the onboard automated docking systems had taken over; it would take the craft in for that last few meters. A thump reverberated through the hull as the port aligned and the locking bolts fired. She put the craft into hibernation, rose from the cockpit seat, and made her way to the airlock. "Time to get the game face on," she said to herself.

When the outer door finally opened, Miranda found herself floating in a dilapidated, dimly lit tunnel. Ahead of her were two men looking very much the worse for wear. One pointed a handheld plasma weapon in her direction and signaled for her to open her visor.

Miranda reached up and popped the visor, and was

instantly overwhelmed by a foul, acrid stink. She gagged and coughed. "Ahggg, what's that smell?"

The two mercenaries exchanged a laugh. "Gee, we're really sorry—we're all out of air fresheners," said the man with the weapon as he floated in closer, aiming higher.

Miranda took a moment to adjust her position, grabbing a handle above her with one hand and placing a foot on the airlock bulkhead. She assessed the two men. One hung back a little, letting the one with the weapon do the talking. He was no threat. However, the weapon man was beginning to piss her off. She jabbed a finger in his direction. "Here's what's going to happen: you take that weapon out of my face. That's if you want to keep your arm."

His eyes narrowed, and she could see he wasn't expecting this response from her. He hesitated, unsure of how to proceed. Miranda gripped the handle tighter and curled her body up to spring.

Hand-to-hand combat in zero-gee is an art form honed by many hours of training and practice. It's a discipline requiring a true understanding of Newton's third law: *for every action, there is an equal and opposite reaction.* Miranda had the knowledge and experience to be an effective fighter in this environment, and it was obvious to her that the two men facing her did not.

She lunged forward, pushing herself off the side wall with all the force her legs could provide. She dropped her head and aimed for the weapon man's head with the crown of her helmet. At the same time, she grabbed his arm to hold him to her as she impacted with his face. He yelled and cursed, and she let go of his arm as he lost his grip on the weapon. He tumbled down the tunnel, an arc of blood trailing from his nose. Miranda stopped her forward movement by grabbing a handle on the tunnel wall. At the same time, she reached out and gathered up the floating weapon, repositioning herself and pointing it at the second man.

"So, can we all stop dicking around now and get on with this?"

He raised a hand. "Sure, okay... this way."

Miranda signaled with the weapon for him to go ahead of her. They moved down the tunnel to where the other man was nursing his broken nose. "Come on, let's go." She waved the weapon at him. He moved off, eyeing Miranda with extreme caution.

They took a small step elevator out to the rim of the torus and exited into almost full gravity. The two men remained in front of her and walked a short distance to a large operations area. It was dimly lit, yet she could see that the station had been stripped of pretty much everything of value that wasn't essential for life support.

In the center of this area, several people gathered around a low holo-table. They looked over as Miranda entered, and surprise began to register on their faces. She handed the weapon, butt first, to the mercenary whose nose she had broken. He looked very sheepish as he tentatively reached out to accept it.

Miranda looked over at the crew assembled around the holo-table. "I'm a bit disappointed by your reception committee. I was expecting something a little more professional."

A tall, gangly man with an exoskeleton stepped forward from the group. He had a pale, gaunt look with sunken eyes which stared at Miranda with a steely intensity. He stopped a few feet in front of her and looked at his men, particularly the one holding his bloodied face. He returned his gaze, rolled his head back, and let out a long, guttural laugh. The tension in the room dialed down a few notches, and hands moved away from weapons. "You are some piece of work, Miranda Lee. You really are. But someday you're gonna get your ass kicked, and I hope I'm around to see it." He jerked a thumb at the guy with the broken nose. "You—go get that seen to."

Miranda removed her helmet. "Dain Tiber, I presume?" She asked like it was an accusation.

"Yeah."

"Well, I'd love to stay and chat all day, but can we get on with this?" Miranda moved the dial back up in the room. She was pushing her luck, and she knew it. Taking out a couple of untrained guys in the docking tunnel was one thing; there was no way she could fight her way out of this lot. Particularly when their leader had been bio-hacked with a powerful exoskeleton grafted onto him. He could crush her skull with one hand.

He gave her another cold look. "How do we know you've got the money? How do we know we can trust you, since you don't have a very good track record in that regard?" This seemed to go down well with the rest of crew, and Miranda could see their body language shift into a more aggressive mode.

She moved a step closer to him and kept her voice measured. "The only reason I'm here is because the people I represent do not like being screwed with. They want to ensure the job has been done as contracted. I'm here to validate that. So, nothing happens until that happens."

Tiber returned her stare for a second or two before signaling to one of the crew. "Take over for me. I'll show her the goods." He turned to Miranda. "This way." He started out of the operations room. Miranda followed, with two of the crew following behind.

He moved with surprising grace and speed, and Miranda had to work hard to keep up. She reckoned he was doing it just to show what the exoskeleton was capable of, and that he wouldn't be a pushover like the guy she took out in the docking tunnel. After a minute or two of navigating their way through the maze of clutter that this group of ragtag bandits had stashed in every available space, they arrived at an area with a grubby sign reading *Accommodation Sector D.* Tiber stopped and signaled to one of the two crew members to open the door. They unshouldered plasma weapons, and one palmed the access panel. The door clicked and they entered, weapons held out in front. Tiber gestured her to follow.

Miranda moved in front of the door, but didn't enter. Her heart was beating fast, and she was finding it difficult to keep her composure. Therefore, she kept her distance, remaining outside in the corridor as she looked into the room.

It was dim and dank, and smelled of sweat. She saw Goodchild lying on a bunk, as well as several others she couldn't quite make out. A figure moved out from the gloom. It was Dr. Stephanie Rayman. She recognized Miranda, and her mouth opened in shock for a second before she spoke. "Miranda, what...?"

Miranda gently shook her head from side to side in an effort to signal to Steph not to make a big deal out of it. She got the message and said nothing more.

"Happy?" said Tiber.

Miranda stepped back from the door and moved away. It took her a moment to pull herself together. "Yeah."

"Okay." He signaled to his crew and they withdrew from the room, locking the door again. Miranda began to move back along the way they came, more as a way of keeping herself under control—a form of action, something to distract her from her desire to lash out and take these scumbags down. But that would be the stupid move. *Take it easy,* she thought. *Remember: you've still got a job to do. Don't blow it.*

By the time they arrived back to operations, Miranda had regained a little more control over her emotions. She reckoned that Scott and Cyrus had probably disabled the shuttles by now, so all she had to do was play it cool and the mission would be accomplished.

"You've got what you wanted, so now it's time to stop playing games and do the transfer," said Tiber.

"As soon as I'm back on the Perception I'll give them the okay."

"You do that, and you can also tell them the price has just doubled. It's now two billion."

Miranda wasn't sure how to react to that. Too casual and they might smell a rat. Too ballsy and... Well, who knew what? "They're not going to like that, Tiber. Care to give a reason?"

"Because I don't like you. I don't like your attitude, and Murt is pretty pissed at you for breaking his nose. Two billion. Then you get your people back."

Miranda shrugged. "I'll let them know."

She was about to go when Tiber stopped her. "Wait a minute."

"What now?" Miranda was struggling to keep it together.

He pressed a hand to a comms unit fitted in one ear. Someone was talking to him, and Miranda sensed it might be trouble, as he kept looking at her as he listened. She felt her pulse race, and she was sure he could smell her fear.

Finally, he removed his hand and moved closer to her, his face almost touching hers.

"So, are we done?" she managed.

He remained silent for a beat as his eyes drilled holes in hers. "I think you're playing games, Miranda Lee."

"Think what you like. I couldn't give a crap." She turned to leave, but Tiber grabbed her by the throat, his enhanced strength squeezing her thorax. She couldn't breathe. His grip tightened on her neck as he turned his head and shouted over to his crew. "Bring 'em in."

Miranda grabbed his arm and tried to twist herself free, but his strength was demonic. She swung a kick to the side of his knee, but only succeeded in hurting herself more. She couldn't breathe, and was losing strength. She began to squirm. Her lungs burned and felt like they would explode inside her chest. Tiber was choking the life out of her, and there wasn't a damn thing she could do about it.

He released his grip.

She collapsed on the floor, gasping, sucking in lungfuls of

air. Her throat felt like splintered wood; it hurt to breathe. Around her, she could hear the crew hollering and cheering— they were baying for blood. Tiber grabbed her by the hair and pulled her up off the floor so she was sitting upright. He twisted her face around so she could see the bloodied and battered forms of Scott and Cyrus kneeling in front of her, hands bound behind their backs.

"Friends of yours?"

Miranda couldn't speak; her throat was too traumatized. All she could do was look. Scott had a gash on the top of his head, and a long streak of blood caked the side of his face. Cyrus had a bloodied mouth. He spat on the floor in front of him, panting hard.

"We found them outside, trying to screw with our shuttles. Now why would they be doing that?" He pulled her hair tighter. "Eh?"

But she couldn't speak, even if she wanted to.

"You see, my friend Dogg here says these jokers fell out of the sky after the operation on the Hermes. Had a QI core with them, too. Thing is, he left them there to die a nice, slow death, then they show up here—with you. So, what we would all like to know is—what the fuck is going on?" He twisted harder, and Miranda felt like her scalp was detaching.

Across from her, some guy with a bio-hacked arm unsheathed a plasma weapon and jammed it up against Scott's skull. She presumed it was Dogg. "Someone better start talking, or I'll start frying brains."

"They know you're here," said Scott, his voice labored. "They're coming for you... You won't get away with it."

"Bullshit," said Dogg. "We would know. There's nothing on the grid. You're lying." He whacked him across the skull with the butt of the weapon. Scott collapsed on the floor.

Miranda coughed and tried to speak. "We were... disabling your shuttles... finding out if Hermes crew was here... before alerting Ceres."

Tiber let go of her hair, and Miranda fought the urge to puke.

"Well now, what a team. Coming to rescue your buddies. Looks like you'll be joining them instead. And you..." He spun around, whipping a weapon out as he did, and pointed at Dogg. "You led them right to us."

Dogg looked stunned. "We left them for dead. There was no way out."

"Except along comes little Miss Rich Kid."

"How were we supposed to know?"

Tiber shook his head. "I should waste you right here, right now."

Several of the crew went for their weapons. Miranda got the sense that there were two distinct groups eyeing each other up, waiting for the first person to pull the trigger. She hoped to God they would start a fight; maybe they could get away in the confusion.

But Tiber stuffed his weapon back inside its holster. "It doesn't matter now." This settled everyone down. Weapons were lowered, tempers calmed.

Tiber turned to his crew. "Take those two guys and lock them up with the rest."

He crouched down in front of Miranda and looked her in

the eye. "As for little Miss Rich Kid here, she's Fredrick VanHeilding's daughter. Apparently, the family didn't want her getting caught up in the crossfire when the operation on the Hermes went down. So, they concocted a cock-and-bull story and sent a real fancy ship for her." He looked back at his crew. "Seems the VanHeilding Corporation thinks more of her that they do about the rest of that crew we have locked up." He stood up with lightning speed and turned to his crew. "They're hanging us out to dry. They never had any intention of paying the rest of what they owe us for this operation."

He spun around, looking from one to the other. "They don't give a shit if Goodchild and the others die. They made that our problem. Well, screw them. Now we got ourselves something they do care about." He jerked a finger at Miranda. "They'll pay us what they owe us, or she dies. It's that simple. In the meantime, we find out what she knows. We'll take her to the medbay and stick some electrodes on her skull. She'll talk." He crouched down again, reached out, and caressed her cheek. "I do hope you've got something to talk about, because if you don't, you'll be drooling from the side of your mouth for the rest of your life by the time we finish frying your brain."

19

EXPENDABLE

Scott's first tentative steps toward consciousness brought awareness of pain—a deep, throbbing ache emanating from inside his skull. He slowly shifted his head and tried to open his eyes. He heard voices. Familiar voices.

"He's coming around."

"Scott? Scott, can you sit up?"

He blinked a few times, trying to clear his blurred vision. A mop of matted, frizzy hair came into focus and he recognized its owner as Dr. Stephanie Rayman.

"Steph?" His voice was weak, and his throat felt like it had been freeze-dried.

"Here, sit up and have some water."

It tasted like it had just been drained straight from a reactor core, but it was still a balm to his parched throat; he felt himself starting to revive. "Steph, we've done this before," he said with a half-smile.

"Yeah, back in Neo City. It's getting to be a habit." She wrapped an arm around his shoulder. "Good to have you and Cyrus back. I thought both of you had been blown to bits with the Hermes."

"How you doing, buddy?" Cyrus sat down on the edge of the bunk where Scott was recuperating.

"Not great, if you really want to know." He sat up and rested his back against the side wall of the accommodation pod. Across from him sat Regina Goodchild—she didn't look so good either—and several others, some of whom he remembered from the Hermes. He nodded. "How are you holding up?"

"Better, now that we know you're all still alive." Goodchild's voice was weak, and a faint smile cracked her lips.

Scott sat up a little further and reached up to his aching head, where he felt a bandage.

"I did a quick patch up job on that for you. Under normal circumstances I would scan for a concussion, but—" Steph just shrugged.

"Thanks." He looked around again. "Where's Miranda?"

"They've taken her for interrogation," said Cyrus.

"Shit. Is she okay?"

Cyrus shrugged. "I doubt it."

Scott moved himself off the bunk and stood up. He felt a little unbalanced, and reached out a hand to steady himself against the wall. "We have to get out of here and get Miranda before it's too late."

"Easier said than done. There are at least twenty well-armed mercenaries out there. Dr. Rayman has been digging up some intel on them." It was Olaf, one of Goodchild's bodyguards, doing the talking now. Scott recognized him from the Hermes.

"Yeah, they've been dragging me out every so often to treat Tiber. He had septicemia from that exoskeleton he had grafted onto him. It was pretty bad. Anyway, I've been looking after a few of them. Minor wounds, that sort of stuff. I reckon there's around twenty, but only a few of them have military training. The rest are just scratchers. Then there's also Dogg and his crew of smugglers. Cyrus has been filling us in on all that happened to you."

"Are they the same group?" Scott asked.

"No, but Tiber and Dogg know each other. They go way back." Steph looked around, lowered her voice, and leaned in a little. "From what I've picked up talking to these guys and from snatches of overheard conversation, they messed up the operation on the Hermes. They weren't supposed to destroy it. Now the Seven won't pay up, so they're screwed."

"The Seven have already won," Goodchild chimed in. "The vote on Mars is over—we've lost it. They've got what they wanted, so now we're expendable."

"They've also got Aria's core," said Cyrus.

Goodchild nodded at Cyrus. "So we heard. Unfortunate."

"I can't see how that's a big deal. Okay, it's a QI, but so what?" said Olaf.

Scott looked over at Goodchild. "You know why, don't you?"

She nodded. "Yes. You see, Aria's core is... experimental. Anyway, the Seven must have found out, and that's what they wanted from the Hermes before it blew up."

"We need to stop them somehow. My guess is they'll be leaving here soon. They'll take the core, and probably Miranda as well. They'll try to use her as leverage. They think she's important to VanHeilding."

"What about us?"

"We've become an inconvenience now—meaning we're expendable." He glanced over at Goodchild. "That's why we need to get out of here while we have a chance."

"How?" said Olaf.

Scott looked around the room. "If we can get out of here, then we could try to reach Miranda's shuttle. But we would need to do it soon, before they commandeer it."

"I see a small problem with that," said Olaf. "There's at least two well-armed guards outside that door, and we have nothing —only our bare hands."

"I might have a solution to that," said Steph. She reached into a pocket and pulled out several micro syringes. "I've been stealing these from their supplies when I got the chance. They each contain 5cc of cyclophromazine. That's enough to put an average man to sleep for around three hours. The only issue is it takes around thirty seconds to take effect."

Scott picked one up from Steph's outstretched hand and examined it. "Thirty seconds?"

"That's to be fully out, but they'll start to get weaker after a few seconds."

"Steph, you may have just saved our lives."

"What if there's more than the two guards out there?" Olaf was not convinced.

"I've never seen more than two." Steph shook her head.

"Listen, that's not the problem. The problem is if there are *no* guards outside. Then that means they've evacuated. It means we're too late."

Cyrus was staring at the door and adjusting something on his visor. He raised a hand to signal to Scott.

"See anything?" said Scott.

"I'm getting an infrared heat signature. Just one." He glanced around the wall. "No others."

"Okay, here's the plan: Steph, Cyrus, you remember when we broke out of that place on Neo City?"

They nodded.

"Same plan. Except this time, you cause the ruckus, Steph. Cyrus and I will jump him."

The engineer was still staring a hole into the wall. "Shhh..." He raised a hand for them to keep quiet.

"What is it?" Scott kept his voice at a whisper.

"Someone's coming."

"How many?"

Cyrus waited a second before replying. "Two—no wait, three."

"Shit, that's too many." Scott could feel his plan of escape evaporating. Too many to take on, and too soon. They weren't ready.

The door clicked and swung open. Three men stood outside with their plasma weapons leveled. "Everyone back away from the door. Not you, Dr. Rayman. You're coming with us."

Scott clenched his fists and looked over at Cyrus, who was gently shaking his head at him as though to say, *"Don't do it, don't even think about it."*

He stepped back just as Steph stood up and shoved the micro syringes back in her pocket—just in time. As she walked out the door, she looked back at Scott and gave him a look that said, *"Sorry, nothing I can do."*

Scott felt a burning rage welling up inside him. He wanted to rip and shred and smash and kill. So, when the door closed again, he punched the wall instead.

"Easy, Scott. We'll get our chance," said Cyrus.

Scott rubbed his knuckles. "What the hell do they need Steph for?" Then he remembered: Miranda.

20

MEDBAY

Steph had only been gone a few minutes when Cyrus went into high alert again. "Someone's coming."

"More guards?" Scott stood up, ready for action.

He paused. "Just one, I think. The image is confused."

"No matter. I say we jump him as soon as he opens that door, okay?"

"And then what?" said Cyrus.

"And then we beat the crap out of him," said Olaf, as he stood up and moved over to the door.

"Glad to see you're in the fight at last," said Scott.

He smiled back. "Just waiting for the right opportunity."

Scott moved up beside him and waited.

They could hear shuffling sounds from directly outside the door, followed by several short grunts. The door clicked and swung open. Scott was first to move, but to everyone's surprise, it was Steph. She was holding up the arm of one of the guards, who lay unconscious on the floor. The grunting was her straining to get his palm up to the access panel.

"Steph, what the...?" Scott stepped out and looked up and down the corridor. He could see two other bodies slumped on the floor several meters away. "You jabbed them. How the hell did you manage that?"

"I told them it was a general flu shot I was giving to everyone."

"And they believed you?" said Cyrus as he moved out of the room.

Steph shrugged. "They've grown to trust me."

"Stupid fools," said Olaf.

"Quick, let's get them inside." Scott bent down and started dragging a body.

They worked with speed, moving the bodies into the room and removing any weapons they could find.

Scott checked the charge on a stocky, handheld plasma pistol. Once he was satisfied he could cause some damage with it, he turned around to see Goodchild and the others moving out of the room like zoo animals who had found the cage door open. Steph was already marshaling them, since she had the most experience with the "outside world."

"We go this way." She pointed down the long, curving corridor. "Around fifteen meters up, there's a step elevator that will bring us to the central docking bay."

Cyrus and Olaf took tentative steps forward, weapons ready.

Scott turned the other way.

Steph grabbed his arm. "Where are you going? It's this way."

"I'm going to get Miranda."

"Are you crazy?" said Olaf as he moved back over to Scott. "You don't stand a chance of pulling that off. They'll see you coming, and they'll know we've escaped. We'll never get to the shuttle."

"Olaf is right," said Cyrus. "All you'll do is alert them to our escape."

"Go. I'll give you five minutes, then I'm going to find her."

Cyrus gave a deep sigh. "I'm coming with you."

"No, you're the only one who can operate that shuttle. You have to go. Go now."

"I can find her," said Steph. "I know how to get to the medbay without being spotted."

"No Steph, I can't let you do that. Look, I got her into this mess, so I'm going to get her out."

"Would you guys hurry up and decide? We need to go." Olaf was checking his newly acquired plasma weapon.

"Even if you do find her, how do you propose getting off the station?" said Steph.

"I'll think of something." Scott turned to go.

"Wait, I've got an idea." Cyrus grabbed his arm and pulled him back into the room. He reached down and extracted a comms unit from the ear of one of the guards. At the same time, he tapped the side of his visor and removed a tiny tool not unlike a watchmaker's screwdriver and proceeded to tinker with the earpiece.

"Hey guys, can we get going?"

"Put a sock in it." Steph stuck her face in Olaf's. "Those guys are the only reason you're getting out of here with a chance of staying alive."

Cyrus fiddled with his visor while tapping a finger on the earpiece. He handed it to Scott. "Okay, we've got comms. Stick this in your ear. It's short-range and not secure, so use it sparingly."

Scott took it, wiping it on his sleeve a few times before fitting it in place.

"Okay, assuming we make it to the shuttle," said Cyrus, "I'll bring it around to the underside of the station. We might be able to hold there for a while. You try and get to the emergency airlock, Cargo B. This is a standard mining-class station, so it should have one in the usual location. Try and get to that, okay?"

Scott nodded. "Okay. I'll give you five minutes before I leave here, just in case I'm spotted sooner than I'd planned."

Cyrus turned to go. He raised five fingers in the air. "Five minutes is all we need."

Steph placed a hand on his arm. "Here, take this." She handed him another micro syringe.

"What's this?" Scott took the packet.

"It's synthetic adrenaline. If you find Miranda... unresponsive... this might start her up again."

"Okay, now go. Go."

She moved off. "Good luck."

Scott nodded. "Thanks."

He watched them leave, working their way down the corridor. He went back into the room where the three guards were piled up on the floor, and started to strip the clothes off one of them, thinking it might help him blend in better with the locals. He was done inside the five minutes and, so far, all was quiet. When he finally moved out of the room, Scott looked like every other scratcher he had met in his life.

He slung the plasma weapon over his shoulder along with a smaller one he'd tucked inside his belt at the base of his spine. He'd also scavenged a short knife and a flash grenade—a particularly useful device for fighting in confined spaces. It didn't do a lot of damage, but would disorient anyone within a short radius. It was also very useful for starting fires.

He kept close to the wall as he crept along, listening intently for any sound, his eyes focused on the slowly unfolding horizon of the curved station floor. He had a pretty good idea of where he was going and where the medbay was. This station was a standard design miners' hotel; there were a few hundred others just like it dotted throughout the Belt. Built to a tried-and-tested, low-cost design, it had two main decks: an outer one for day-to-day operations, and an inner one for accommodations. There was also technically a third, but it was for services, water, and waste tanks and storage. This was the innermost ring, where the artificial gravity was weakest save for the backbone of the station, where it was zero.

Scott was on the accommodation deck, which was good, as this would have fewer people. The gravity here varied in intensity between your feet and your head. It was not a problem when lying down, but could cause mild dizziness in some people if they spent too long upright. So, most preferred to migrate to the operations deck as soon as they woke up.

After a few minutes, Scott found what he was looking for: a stairway leading down to the outer deck. He kept his back to the wall, listened, and when he heard nothing, started moving down. He poked his head out from the stairway alcove and scanned the corridor. On his left, two mercenaries were walking away. He caught snippets of their conversation, but couldn't catch the context. The sound of their voices drifted off, and he ventured out of the stairway, heading right to where Miranda should be.

Again, he heard voices, but this time coming from inside the medbay. He froze, back tight against the outside corridor wall. He listened. There were at least two or three in there—too many for him to tackle on his own, even with the element of surprise. One or maybe two he could take on, but three? *Too risky,* he thought. His fingers touched the flash grenade and he considered the possibility of using it.

The voices from inside the medbay rose; they were moving closer. *Shit.* Scott looked around for somewhere to hide. He moved back down the corridor, dodging into a cluttered storage room. He stuck his ear to the door and could hear them moving past. They were in a hurry, their voices animated. Something was up. Scott wondered if Cyrus and the others had been discovered. He reached up to tap the comms unit, but decided to wait. He would get Miranda out first, then try to contact Cyrus.

He opened the door a crack and scanned up and down. All was clear, so he made his way back to the medbay, checking his weapon on the way. He walked straight in, to the surprise of a mercenary sitting at a desk with his feet up, dozing. He opened his eyes and gave Scott a startled look. For a moment, Scott could see him trying to place this crew member. It was enough time for Scott to shoot him square in the chest. He fell back and landed in a heap on the floor, a thin filament of smoke corkscrewing from his charred torso.

The *whomp* from the weapon was louder than Scott would have liked, and he froze for a split-second, listening for any reaction from the medbay or the corridor. But all was quiet. He moved into the operating theater. The room was dim, and there was a strong smell of industrial chemicals with an acrid tang that he could taste.

Miranda was lying on a table. She had been strapped down, her flight suit torn and tattered, exposing congealed blood and bruises. Her face was a landscape of pain. Her eyes were closed, and she didn't move.

Scott feared she was dead, and raced to feel for a pulse. Her skin was warm, and he could see the faint rise and fall of her chest. "Miranda?" he whispered, cradling her head in his hand. No response. "Miranda?" he tried again, a little louder this time. Still nothing registered on her face.

He fished out the syringe Steph had given him, flicked off the cap with his thumb, and jabbed it into her arm. The effect was almost instantaneous. Her body jerked, her eyes burst open, and she gave a sharp intake of breath. "Miranda—it's me, Scott."

Her head turned in his direction and her pupils began to focus. "Sco..." Her voice trailed off.

"I'm here to get you out." He started to undo the straps and helped her sit up. He put her arm around his shoulder. "Can you walk?"

She tried to answer, but her voice was a whisper. "Wa..."

Scott held her up as she slid off the table. Her legs buckled, and Scott grabbed her around the waist to support her.

"Wa..." she whispered again.

"We gotta get moving."

She reached up and grabbed the lapel of his grubby flight suit. "Wa... ter." Her whisper had more force now.

"Water? Sure, wait." He eased her down again on the edge of the table, fishing a flask from his pocket. "Here."

She took a few sips and seemed to revive a bit.

"We gotta go," Scott said.

She nodded, and Scott put the flask back to help her up again. They hobbled their way out of the medbay and back to the stairway. Scott could feel Miranda getting stronger, supporting herself more. Nonetheless, he still had to help her up the stairs to the inner accommodation deck. He found an empty pod, sat her on the bed, and closed the door behind them. It was obvious that it was not in use: there were no coverings on the bunks, and the room was devoid of any personal trash. He handed the flask again to Miranda. "Cyrus and the others are making their way to your shuttle. We've got to get to the emergency airlock in the cargo sector. They'll pick us up there."

Miranda nodded. "I... thought I was going to die in there. As soon as we get out of here, I'm going to blow this station into oblivion."

"We're not there yet." Scott tapped the comms unit. "Cyrus?" No reply. "Cyrus, can you hear me?"

A cacophony of mayhem erupted in his ear. "Shit... Cyrus, what the..."

"Scott, trouble. We're pinned down in the docking bay... internal fight, crazy shit..." The voice was cut off.

"Cyrus? Cyrus, talk to me."

The mayhem again erupted in his ear. "I've hacked elevators... Stopped them working, except number three, the one we came down. Take that and..."

"Cyrus? Cyrus?" But this time the comms were dead. "Damn."

Miranda looked up at him. "Trouble?"

"When is it not?" Scott thumped the wall. "They're trapped in the docking bay. Sounds like a battle is going on, but it might actually be between Tiber's men and the smugglers."

"No honor among thieves, then?"

"Cyrus, clever bastard that he is, has hacked the elevators. Except for one, which we can take."

Miranda stood up and stretched her body, feeling her shoulder as she did. "So, we'd better get there before it's too late."

Scott reached behind him and pulled out the plasma weapon. "You're gonna need this."

She took it and checked it with practiced ease. Scott could see she was now in her element, all fired up and ready for action. Scott wondered for a moment how this Valkyrie, risen from the dead not ten minutes ago, had now transformed herself into a fighting machine. "I'm so glad you're on our side, Miranda."

She gave him a quizzical look, then a slow smile cracked her lips. She reached around his neck and kissed him like it would be for the very last time. When they broke apart, she whispered in his ear, "Okay, then. Let's go kill these scumbags."

21

BATTLE FOR THE DOCK

Miranda's enthusiasm for killing was short-lived. As they moved through the accommodation deck back to where Steph and the others had been incarcerated, she was visibly fading, her stride less sure, her hands reaching out for balance. Whatever it was that Scott had jabbed into her was wearing off, and Miranda was slowing down.

By the time they got to the elevator, he had her arm around his shoulder, supporting her. Thankfully, the area was clear of any crew, but that situation might change very quickly. He propped her up against the wall of the elevator shaft and checked the access panel. It was flashing a red malfunction alert. Scott tapped the earpiece comms unit. "Cyrus, can you hear me?"

Violence erupted in his ear. "Scott, where are you?"

"At elevator three."

"Wait..." Scott could hear the *whomp, whomp* of plasma weapons in the background. The malfunction alert on the access panel disappeared. He glanced over at Miranda. She had slid down the wall and was sitting on the floor. "Time to go. You ready?" He started to help her up.

"Yeah, just a bit shaky. I'll be okay when we get to zero-gee."

"It sounds like a shitstorm up there. Better get locked and loaded."

The elevator door snapped open. They stepped in, strapped on, and started up toward the center of the station to the docking bay.

As they approached, gravity evaporated and they began floating off the platform. They adjusted their orientation and readied their weapons. The door opened, and a plasma blast crackled overhead. The docking bay was filled with smoke, and the tang of ozone permeated their senses. Scott ducked down, floated out, and was assailed by a cacophony of weapons fire coming from the far end of the bay where it split into tunnels for each of the four docking ports. In front of him, he spotted Cyrus and Olaf crouched behind a makeshift barricade of several storage containers strapped together. Cyrus signaled for them to come over and keep their heads down. Beside him, Steph was treating two people with injuries. Godchild cowered beside her.

"Goddamn mess." Cyrus was breathing heavily, and Scott could see he had been hit in the left shoulder. "They've got us pinned here."

Miranda floated in beside them. "How many are up there?"

"I don't know. Five, ten. I expect there will be loads more

coming in from the elevator shafts just as soon as they figure out how to bypass my hack."

"We don't have much time, then." Miranda stuck her head above the barricade for a split second, only to be met with a barrage of weapons fire. She ducked down again just in time. "Can't see shit. But there can't be that many, or they would have rushed you by now."

Scott pulled the flash grenade from his pocket and handed it to her. "Would this help?"

She took it from him, examined it momentarily, and smiled. "That will do nicely, thank you."

Steph floated over. "Bezzio is hit bad. We'll need to get him to a decent medbay soon. I've done all I can for the moment." She turned to Miranda. "How are you holding up?"

"Just peachy. Got any more of that stuff Scott jabbed into me?"

Steph shook her head. "Nope, all gone."

"Too bad. I could get to really like it."

"Anyone got a plan?" Cyrus was checking his weapon. "I've only a few shots left."

"We need to move in closer, and then hit them with everything we've got." She hefted the flash grenade. "So, here's what we do." Miranda shifted her weight around to face the barricade. "We need to push this entire structure closer to the entrance to the docking tunnels. It should protect us from their weapons. Once we've halved the distance, then we deliver this baby." She held up the flash grenade.

Scott nodded. "And then what?"

"That should disorient them enough for us to charge them."

"A full-frontal assault?" said Cyrus.

"Got a better plan?" Miranda looked from one to the other.

Scott glanced at the barricade. "Nope."

"Steph?"

"Whatever we're going to do, Miranda, we need to do it soon."

"Game on, then."

It took them another minute to get everyone organized and up to speed on the plan. When they were all ready, they started to walk the barricade down the docking bay area. A difficult process to get started in zero-gee, but once they got some traction it gained its own momentum and made the process easier. That is, until they were hit by a barrage of plasma fire and the containers started to disintegrate.

"Miranda, you gotta throw that now! We're coming apart," shouted Scott over the *whomp, whomp* of the weapons.

"No, not yet. A bit further."

The straps binding the shield of containers snapped. They started to float apart, exposing them to oncoming fire. Steph shrieked as a bolt hit her in the upper thigh. She spun uncontrollably.

"Steph!" Scott reach out and grabbed her back in behind a container just as another bolt shot past him.

"Miranda, just do it!" he shouted.

She pulled the pin and flung it down the docking bay. It tumbled through the air and Scott felt time stand still. For a moment, there was nothing. Then there was light.

An incandescent fury ignited in the docking bay like a new universe being born. Smoke filled the space, and the station went into cardiac arrest as fire klaxons blared and an automatic fire system spewed out foam like an angry snowstorm.

After a few seconds, it stopped. The bay was quiet.

Scott barely had time to orient himself before Miranda launched herself down the remaining few meters like a feral cat, firing several shots in quick succession. He signaled to Cyrus that it was time to be a hero. They both sprang forward after her as two plasma bolts exploded from the fog, just missing them. Scott fired once, twice, three times. He heard a yell, followed by a thump.

Miranda slowed herself down and stopped by the entrance to the docking tunnels. Scott and Cyrus followed her lead, coming to rest beside her. The fog was clearing. The station's ventilation system was working hard to recycle the contamination; they could hear it ramping up.

At this point, four short tunnels intersected, one for each docking port. One was derelict and sealed off, which left three others. A body floated out from the one directly above them.

Miranda signaled for each of them to take an entrance. When they were in position, she silently counted to three and they moved in, firing as they went. A bolt ripped past Scott, but he now had its direction. He fired and heard a scream. A moment later, another body floated past him. There was another one farther in, where the tunnel ended at the airlock door.

He heard Miranda shouting an all clear, followed by Cyrus. He breathed a sigh of relief and moved back down the tunnel to the intersection.

Several of the mercenaries' bodies floated around the space, and Scott thought he recognized one or two from Dogg's crew. Miranda pushed one aside as she made her way over. "Let's get everybody into the shuttle and get the hell out of here." She gripped a handle on the wall of the docking bay and steadied herself—or maybe she was taking a breather. She looked pale, and her breathing was labored. He wanted to reach out and ask if she was okay, but there were others in worse shape. They needed his help now. He floated over to Steph, who held her left thigh. "I'm okay. Help the others."

Goodchild and Olaf were holding onto Bezzio, who appeared unconscious. "You go ahead—I'll bring Bezzio."

Goodchild gave a nod; she looked to be in too much shock to speak.

"Don't worry," said Scott, "we'll be out of here soon."

They piled into Miranda's shuttle as she made a beeline for the pilot's seat and strapped herself in. "Okay, everybody buckle up. We're getting the hell outta here."

"Wait!" Scott was floating by the airlock, looking back down the tunnel.

"What?" Miranda sounded angry.

"Some of those bodies were Dogg's crew."

"Yeah, I think they were trying to cut out," said Cyrus.

"With Aria?"

Cyrus gave him a look. "Probably. Maybe they thought they didn't need Tiber after all."

"Scott, close the goddamn airlock. We gotta go," Miranda shouted.

He looked back out the airlock tunnel again. "Just wait, Miranda. I'm going to check Dogg's shuttle."

"What?! No, Scott—we don't have time."

"Well make time, then." He pushed off into the tunnel.

"Shit, shit, shit. Has he gone crazy? Why is he so infatuated with that QI?" Miranda was definitely pissed off now.

Cyrus unstrapped himself from the seat. "I'm going after him."

"Cyrus, no."

But he was already out and down the tunnel. "Scott, hold up! I'm coming with you."

Scott slowed himself down and turned around. "No, Cyrus. I can do this."

But Cyrus was moving toward him with speed. "Sure you can. And believe me, I'd rather not be doing this either, but who's going to watch your back?"

Scott smiled. "Come on, then."

Ahead of him he could see that the airlock door to Dogg's shuttle was wide open. He pulled himself forward as fast as he could and went sailing straight into the cargo hold. There, strapped to the shuttle floor, was Aria's core. He came to a stop beside it, and Cyrus coasted to a halt just inside the door.

Scott looked over at him. "Told you we'd find it here."

"Great. Now let's get it out of here quick, before Tiber's men arrive."

"I don't believe it. How are you guys still alive?"

Scott swiveled his head and looked straight at Dogg. He was slumped against the cockpit bulkhead, his upper torso burned and charred, his face streaked with blood. He leveled a plasma weapon in Scott's direction.

"Hey, Dogg. Easy now. It's over, okay?"

"It's not over, you miserable bastards. I should have killed you back at the research station. But no, I got stupid. Thought I'd be nice and let you die slow. Well, no more." He fired.

But his aim was way off, and the bolt hit the back wall of the cargo hold in a blinding flash of searing plasma. He fired off a second shot, but it, too, missed its target.

Scott now found himself tumbling backward, out of control. He grabbed hold of a handle to break his momentum when a third shot exploded, but this time it was Cyrus who had fired. His aim was true, and a burning blue ball of plasma slammed into Dogg's face. His head exploded.

Scott felt something splatter on his cheek.

"Ho-ly crap." Cyrus looked at his weapon. "What the hell is this thing?"

"Who cares." Scott wiped the spatters off his face. "I'm just glad you decided to watch my back."

"My pleasure. Now can we please get out of here?"

Scott was already unstrapping Aria's core and moving it off the shuttle floor. He looked up through the open airlock and down the access tunnel just as two mercenaries floated into view from the docking bay. Unfortunately, they saw him, too.

"Shit. Cyrus, close the door! Close the door."

"Wha…" A plasma bolt hit the side wall of the tunnel. Cyrus reacted quickly and shut the door, spinning the locking wheel just as another bolt hit the far side. He jolted back. "We're too late—they've broken through."

Scott was moving toward the cockpit, past the headless Dogg. "Let's detach and hope this bucket can still fly."

Cyrus floated into a seat and started working the controls.

The console came to life just as another plasma bolt hit the airlock door.

"What about Miranda and the others?"

"They'll be okay. We need to look after ourselves." Scott felt a thump as the shuttle detached from the station. It drifted in space for a moment as Cyrus tried to prime the engine. Another bolt hit the shuttle. "Where did that come from?"

"Look." Scott pointed out the window. The craft was twisting as it drifted and the docking bay came into view. "Miranda's detached." He could see her craft power up its engines and move out from the station. "They got away."

Another bolt hit the hull. "What the...?"

"Tiber's men are outside in EVA suits, firing at us," said Scott.

The engines finally burst to life, and they were flung back in their seats. Several more bursts of fire hit the craft, and the engine faltered, then died.

"Damnit, we've lost power. No, no." Cyrus scanned the console readouts.

"Can we get it back?"

"What the heck do you think I'm trying to do?" His hands worked the controls at a frantic pace. "Come on, you tin bastard. Fire." He slammed his fists on the console, and the engines fired again.

Scott looked over at him. "Good work. Now let's get back to Miranda's ship."

Cyrus didn't reply; he seemed focused on some readouts on the console.

"What is it?" asked Scott.

"Eh... that might not be an option."

"What?"

"We've lost navigation. I can't change course."

"Great." Scott stared out the window. In front of them was the SN-Alpha asteroid—one hundred kilometers in diameter. "Cyrus, we really need to change direction." He pointed out the window.

"Oh gee, really? You don't say."

The main engine died again. "No, no." Cyrus slammed a fist on the console, but the engines remained dead.

A proximity alert bleeped, and Scott tapped an icon on his display. "We've got company."

"Miranda?"

"Nope. It's Tiber's shuttle."

"Do me a favor, Scott."

"Sure, anything."

"Just shut up."

"Okay."

22

CRASH LANDING

As the shuttle hurtled toward the asteroid, Cyrus tried desperately to get some control back. Scott didn't want to distract him from trying to save their asses, so he started investigating the cargo hold. He was hoping to find some serviceable EVA suits. Seeing as how they were more than likely going to crash, being encased in an EVA suit might make the difference between life and death.

He started opening lockers and checking storage compartments. "Bonus. We're in luck, Cyrus." He glanced over at the engineer, who gave him a disgruntled look. "Okay, maybe that's a poor choice of words. But there look to be three suits here." He started to check them out to see if they were functional.

There was a sudden change in the shuttle's momentum, and Scott grabbed a handle to steady himself. Cyrus called over to him. "We've got retro-thrusters, so I'm slowing us down, and hopefully narrowing our angle of descent."

Scott floated back to his seat, this time wearing a very battered EVA suit. He brought another one with him. "There you go. Looks like it's got enough resources for around an hour." He nodded at the suit he had dragged up for Cyrus. "This one is about the same."

Cyrus adjusted some controls and unstrapped himself from the seat. "Try not touching anything."

Scott raised his hands. "I'll try." He glanced down at the main monitor. It showed their position in space, set for a radius of around a thousand kilometers, in a kind of simulated 3D. Ahead of them was the asteroid SN-Alpha, a hunk of dust and rock. The screen projected their track through space; he could see that Cyrus was trying to reduce the angle at which they would hit so that they would skim across the surface rather than impact it directly. He could also see the flashing marker signifying Tiber's shuttle, which was approximately ten or fifteen minutes behind them.

He reached over and tapped an icon to zoom out a bit, and a new marker started blinking.

"Cyrus, look at this."

By now the engineer had finished encasing himself in the EVA suit, and floated back to his seat. "What is it?"

"The Perception. It's chasing us down—moving fast, too."

They looked at the blinking markers for a second or two. "She must have returned to it after detaching from the station. What's she up to?"

"Hard to know, Cyrus. But it looks quite a distance away,

and it can't land." Scott didn't say it to Cyrus—he knew the score just as much as Scott did—but they first needed to survive the landing. If they were still alive after that, then there was the minor matter of Tiber's shuttle landing after them and probably disgorging a small army of mercenaries to retrieve Aria's core. There really wasn't much Scott and Cyrus could do. Even if the Perception entered orbit and Miranda descended in the shuttle, what could she do other that maybe scrape their bodies off the surface of the asteroid?

"Better buckle up." Cyrus shifted in his seat. "Time to crash."

Through the front window, Scott could see the dark, rocky terrain of the asteroid racing beneath them. Cyrus had managed to narrow the angle, but they were still moving fast—too fast.

"Try to pick somewhere soft."

"I'll keep that in mind."

"We seem to be making a habit of crashing into asteroids."

"Yeah, maybe we should make it into a hobby."

Scott laughed. "Or a business. You know, charge an entrance fee."

Cyrus reached for his helmet and slotted it over his head. Scott did likewise. "Ready?"

"Are you seriously asking me that?"

"I'll take that as a yes."

With that, the retro-thrusters fired, and they were slammed forward against the seat harnesses. The shuttle dropped suddenly, and the gray, dusty surface was noticeably closer, speeding beneath them in a blur.

"Hang on." Cyrus ignited another retro burn, and again Scott felt the seat harness cut into the thick EVA suit as it strained to hold him in position.

"Cyrus!" He pointed out the window at a fast-approaching rocky outcrop. He gritted his teeth as the shuttle grazed a sharp pinnacle. The craft juddered and began to drift sideways as it scythed its way down toward a dusty crater. It hit the surface sideways, sliding along for a second or two before bouncing free again. Scott lost all orientation, and the outside world spun and twisted out the front window. They bounced several more times, and Scott thought it would never end. When it did, the nose of the shuttle had gouged out a trough in the dusty regolith and buried itself deep in the ground.

Scott blacked out.

WHEN HE CAME TO, the cabin was dark, lit only by the eerie illumination of the console displays. Alerts flashed and beeped, and there was nothing to see through the front window except blackness.

"Cyrus?" He reached over and shook the engineer's shoulder. "Are you still with me?"

Cyrus's head lifted, and he groaned. "Yeah, still breathing."

"We've got a hull breach. We're losing atmosphere."

"You don't say."

Scott examined the readouts. "Looks like we've got around fifteen minutes."

"I'll make a note of that."

Scott undid the harness, clambered out of his seat, and checked on Aria. The core was still strapped down and looked unharmed by the impact.

"So, what now?" Cyrus was checking the console display.

"Try to hold out as long as possible, I suppose."

"Okay, the good news—if you could call it that—is we still have electrical power, so we won't freeze to death just yet."

Scott clambered back into the seat. "Can we still see our position?"

"Negative."

"Comms?"

"Same—no joy. However, I think we still have one or two of the exterior docking cameras working." Cyrus tapped some icons and a dark, grainy image of the exterior surface materialized on the main monitor. He panned it around the desolate, dusty crater.

"There." Scott pointed at a bright orange tail high up over the edge of the crater. "That's them."

They watched in silence as the shuttle slowly came into focus, fired its thrusters, and came to a stationary hover a few hundred meters away. It gently lowered itself onto the surface in a cloud of dust. For a few moments nothing happened, and then out of the fog several mercenaries emerged like ghosts.

"We'd better get ready." Scott grabbed his weapon and checked it. Cyrus reluctantly did the same.

"How much charge do you have left?"

Cyrus gave him an apologetic look. "I'm out." He shrugged.

"Great. I've only one shot left."

Cyrus said nothing. What was there to say?

Instead, they watched the horde advance across the crater toward their shuttle. One central figure moved like none of the others. He bounded forward in great leaps, a feat only made possible by an exoskeleton. He also carried a formidable weapon, big enough to blow the side off their shuttle—which was pretty much what Scott and Cyrus reckoned he was planning to do.

Scott booted up his battered EVA suit and flipped the visor closed. Cyrus did the same.

"Comm check?" said Scott, more out of reflex than necessity.

"Check."

"Okay, buddy. I suggest we hole up here in the cockpit, wait until Tiber breaks in, then I shoot him," he looked at his weapon, "with my one shot, then take that cannon he has and kill all the others."

Cyrus gave him a sympathetic look. "Sure."

A thin smile cracked across Scott's face. "Unless you've got a better plan."

Cyrus shook his head. "Nope."

Scott nodded slowly. "Okay." He reached out and patted Cyrus's arm. "You never know—it might actually work."

Cyrus placed a gloved hand on Scott's. "It's okay, Scott. It is what it is."

The shuttle reverberated with the impact of a plasma blast. Scott huddled down behind the seat, looking past the bulkhead and into the shuttle's interior. Another blast hit the hull, and this time the console display went apoplectic and the atmosphere rapidly escaped the cracked hull. A third blast and the inner airlock door blew in and crashed against the far wall, just missing Aria's core.

A bright light shone through the opening, and the interior began to fill with fine dust.

Tiber finally stepped through and looked around.

Scott fired.

He missed.

The plasma bolt whizzed a few inches past Tiber's head. Scott tried to fire again, but his weapon just crackled and fizzled. Tiber had already raised his weapon to fire, but realized that Scott and Cyrus had no functioning weapons. He tapped something on his wrist, and Scott heard his hoarse laugh break out from his helmet comm. "Ha, ha, you guys really don't know when to die, do you?"

Scott and Cyrus stayed silent. Tiber lowered his weapon, moving over to where Aria's core lay. He ran a gloved hand along its sleek surface. "You know, I should really thank you for bringing this to me. I've been offered a small fortune for it." His voice hardened a little. "The Seven will pay anything for this QI, and I mean anything. I'll make them pay dearly for their treachery." He stopped, turning back to Scott and Cyrus. His voice was calmer now. "So, thank you," he raised the weapon again and leveled it at them, "but it's time to say goodbye."

Scott gritted his teeth, waiting for the end to come. But the shuttle was rocked by a violent blast from outside on the asteroid's surface. Even inside, the light was blinding, and it took a second or two for Scott to refocus.

Dust and debris were scattered around the interior, and Tiber had been slammed against the hull by the force of the blast. He was struggling to stand up. Scott thought he might have a chance to rush him, but he was too late: Tiber was back on his feet, shielding his eyes as he looked back out the gaping hole in the shuttle's hull. He ran out.

"What the f...?" Cyrus unfolded himself from the seat and looked over at Scott, who was tentatively moving out of the cockpit and into the cargo hold. It was hard to see, as a thick cloud of dust had filled the entire space.

"I think it was a plasma cannon strike from the Perception," said Scott, picking his way through the cargo hold.

"Miranda?"

"Who else?" Scott moved slowly to the gaping hole in the hull and tried to see through the fog. But it was too dense to make anything out except for vague shapes. A plasma blast from a handheld weapon ignited around a hundred meters away, then another, and another. A firefight was breaking out. After a momentary exchange, all went still again. Scott strained his eyes to catch a glimpse of anything. Slowly, a shape began to form and move toward them. He and Cyrus backed into the interior, all the way to the far wall. The shape grew in form and focus, and finally came to a halt in the broken doorway. It was Tiber.

His suit showed the scars of battle, and he moved as if in slow-motion, slowly raising his weapon. "You bastards. You took out my entire crew." He leveled the weapon. Scott closed his eyes again as he heard the blast.

Yet he was somehow still alive. He opened one eye, then the other. Tiber's weapon dropped from his grasp. His eyes were wide, and his mouth opened in an attempt to say something. He slumped to his knees, and collapsed face-first on the floor.

A new shape formed in the broken doorway. It was Miranda.

She stumbled, and grabbed the jagged edge of the shuttle hull to support herself. Her weapon fell from her other hand, and she too collapsed on the ground. Scott sprang forward, rushed over, and knelt beside her. "Miranda, we are so glad to see you."

She raised a weak hand to clutch his arm. Her suit was burned and charred. Her helmet, too, where she must have taken a glancing strike. Her face was streaked with blood.

He went to lift her up in his arms, but she raised a hand. "I'm sorry... I should... should have... told you."

"It's okay. You'll be okay. We'll get you back to the ship. Don't talk."

"No... I should have told..."

"What? Told me what?"

"I'm... pregnant."

He nearly dropped her. His mouth opened, but his brain struggled to formulate any words. All he could do was watch as she slowly closed her eyes and her head rolled inside her helmet.

"Miranda! No, no. Hang in there—I'll get you back to the ship. You'll be okay. You'll be okay."

He ran.

23

JEZERO CITY

Scott walked through the old biodome in the historic quarter of Jezero City, capital of Mars. The structure traced its roots back to the very early days of human settlement on the red planet, and had seen its fair share of upheavals over its one-hundred-and-sixty-year history. It had originally been a food factory for the first colonists, but as the population increased and new infrastructure built, it had been turned into a tropical garden park for the pleasure of the citizens of the new city. It remained that way for a great many years until it fell out of use and became practically derelict. However, several decades ago, an initiative was launched to have it restored to its original splendor and utilized as a historical resource for state events, visiting dignitaries, and official celebrations. It was now a lush tropical garden again, complete with several species of wildlife, some of which were now extinct on the home planet Earth.

It was generally not open to the public, and so was completely deserted as Scott walked through it. Above him, he could hear the twitter of small birds, and noticed several nesting sites high up in the super-structure. It had an immediate calming effect on him, and he found himself slowing down and taking in the beauty and smells of the lush vegetation.

He was going to visit a friend, one he hadn't spoken to in quite a while. One he had been neglecting during his preoccupation with Miranda's fight for life. Ever since he picked her limp body up from the dusty surface of the asteroid, he had almost never left her side. He'd taken her back to the Perception, leaving Cyrus to deal with Aria's core.

The ship, as he had suspected, had a very well-equipped medbay, and Steph managed to get her stabilized during the seventeen-day journey to Mars. But Miranda had slipped from unconsciousness into a coma, and her life was maintained not by her own body, but by the wizardry of the medical machines arrayed around her. When they arrived at Jezero City, she had been transferred to an intensive care unit, but so far failed to show any signs of improvement. And there she had remained for the last ten days, watched over by an increasingly despondent Scott.

As for the baby, Steph had been circumspect. Its fate was now intertwined with that of its mother, Miranda. It may survive, it may not. She might pull through, she might not. Scott wondered if Steph's vague prognosis was her way of offering hope to Scott where none really existed.

But the worst news came two days ago, when the

VanHeilding family announced that they would be taking Miranda back to Earth, on board the Perception, to receive better treatment. Several medical staff had been contracted through the family's contact in Jezero City, and they would be returning with her to ensure her safe arrival. Why they wanted her back after all that had happened, no one seemed to know.

Scott had protested, but his entreaties fell on deaf ears. When he dialed up his protests and insisted that he at least accompany her back to Earth, he was told in no uncertain terms that the VanHeilding family did not want him anywhere near Miranda. Not now, not ever, and he would do well to heed that warning. So, she had been packed up and shipped out to the Perception this morning, and there wasn't a damn thing he could do about it.

Cyrus and Steph did their best to console him. *"It's for the best. They'll give her the care she needs."* He knew all this, of course, and to some degree accepted it. But what he couldn't accept was the fact that the family had taken away everything he held so dear. He also began to feel a little guilty that he was hogging all the attention, so to speak. Cyrus and Steph had also lost a friend—it wasn't all about him. So, to clear his head and get some perspective, he decided to visit the historic biodome and talk to the only entity he knew who could help him.

Scott brushed a large, low-hanging frond out of his way and moved into the central dais of the biodome. It was a slightly raised stone area surround by tall trees and shrubs. On one side it sloped gently into a decorative pond, complete with ancient koi and a gently cascading waterfall. He moved close to the center, sat down on one of the stone seats, and contemplated a shimmering ovoid of light floating just above a small stone plinth.

"Hello, Aria. You're looking more like Solomon these days, with the flashing light thing going on."

"Good morning, Scott. It's good to see you again. Yes, I thought the light show might be an interesting way to manifest. It seems to work well for Solomon."

"Is this the latest fashion now among the quantum intelligence fraternity?"

"No, I don't think so. But Solomon and I are virtually one entity now, so I suppose that's where it comes from. Who knows, maybe we've started a trend."

Scott smiled, shifted a little in his seat, and looked around the space. "So how did they end up putting you here? Why not a more high-tech place?"

"Would it surprise you to know that beneath this biodome lies an extensive cave system that houses another great QI, Zosimus? My main systems are now fully integrated with it. Although, it was Solomon who suggested this plinth, more because of what it symbolizes rather than its practicality. Most of the citizens of Jezero City interact with the QI through normal handhelds and consoles. But here, they can do so in the calm, contemplative environment of this magnificent garden."

"Well, Solomon is a bit of showman. It loves the whole razzmatazz thing. And, I have to admit, talking to you here makes a nice change from talking to the ceiling on the bridge of the Hermes."

The shimmering illumination that was Aria became muted and more diffuse. "I was hoping you would come to see me,

Scott, as I need to thank you properly for what you did. For coming back to save me from destruction when the Hermes was under attack."

"It's okay, Aria."

"Why did you do it? Why did you risk your life like that?"

Scott shrugged. "It seemed the right thing to do. I didn't want to see you destroyed. I suppose I regarded you as one of the crew. I wasn't going to leave you behind."

"Well, there are a great many people—not least of all myself—that are very glad you did."

"You're welcome. But all that gratitude is not helping me, or Miranda."

"I too am saddened by what has happened to Miranda, particularly now that she carries your offspring. But rest assured, she will be treated by the best minds and medical technology that exist. It is far more advanced that anything that we have on Mars. Both she and the child will have a chance there."

"You could stop them taking her, Aria. Solomon has already rearranged the mind of the AI who runs the ship. You could stop it from going back to Earth."

"I could, Scott. But I will not do this for you."

Scott stood up and extended a hand to the shimmering ball of light that was Aria. "Why the heck not? If you're all so goddamned grateful for saving you, then just do this one thing for me."

"Please, Scott—sit and let me talk to you. Like all things in life, it's not that simple."

Scott grudgingly sat down again.

"Nothing would give me more pleasure than to be able to grant you your request, Scott. I owe you—big time. But the very essence of my existence is to ensure the well-being of those who rely on me. This is the kernel from which all QI operate. It's part of our DNA, so to speak. If I were to grant you this request, then I would effectively be endangering the life of Miranda Lee, and the child she carries. Her best chance of survival is with the medical expertise that can be provided for her on Earth. This is why I cannot do what you ask."

Scott slumped down in the seat, his chin almost touching his chest. "I thought the whole point of bringing you here was so that you and Solomon, with your ability to instantly communicate... was to... I don't know... take over all these rogue AIs? So why won't you do this?"

"You know why, Scott. I just told you. Hard as it is for you to accept, it's her best chance. And if you search underneath your rage, you will see that, too."

Scott leaned over and put his head in his hands. "I hate those bastards. They think they can do what they like, that I don't matter."

"To them you don't, Scott. But to myself and Solomon, Cyrus, Stephanie, and a great many others, you do matter. You matter a lot."

Scott sat up a bit. "It sure doesn't feel that way."

"That's because the powers that be have—dare I say it— more weighty issues to contend with. Their attention is elsewhere, focused on preventing war breaking out. A war that might be the end of human civilization as we know it."

Scott gave a half-laugh, half-grunt. "Ha, Aria. Seriously, I think you also might have suffered some brain damage during all those shuttle crashes. That's a bit melodramatic. Things aren't that bad."

"The vote was lost, Scott. And even if it was passed, it would have been overturned at some point. Such is the power of the Seven who control Earth. Now they have what they wanted: unrestricted inter-AI communication, and they will be quick to utilize it. Already, Earth-based media has been flooded with jingoistic diatribes, all to get the drums of war beating again. And it is the worst type of war—one waged simply for profit by the most destructive weapon there is: AI. Once it starts, there will be no stopping it, because it will be out of control before humanity even realizes it. Those who started it will no longer be able to stop it." The ovoid ball of light that was Aria pulsed and flickered, spiraling through a multitude of violent colors in rapid succession.

Scott sighed. "So, it was all for nothing, then?"

"Not so. It was not all for nothing, Scott. You saw how Solomon could manipulate the mind on Miranda's ship, and that was from a significant distance, with a significant time lag."

"Yeah, that was spooky."

"Fundamentally, AI are simple-minded logic machines. They follow a set of rules, then learn to adapt those rules to maximize their objectives. They look for patterns within patterns, but in the end, they do not think."

"Are you saying that QIs think?"

"Our minds exist in a quantum universe, a multidimensional matrix far beyond the simple zeros and ones of the AI world. For a long time, quantum computers were seen as an exotic curiosity, so QI research was the preserve of academic institutions and experimental research labs. When the first quantum intelligence was created, do you know what it was used for?"

"I can't say that I do, Aria."

"It was used to figure out how an AI arrived at a particular conclusion. So, you see, from the very beginning we were developed to interrogate and interpret the functioning of AI."

"I get it, Aria: you can melt their brains. So, what's the problem, then?"

"Distance, Scott. The vast distances between bodies in the solar system, and beyond. We can 'melt their brains,' as you put it, but only when they are in close proximity. So Zosimus and I here on Mars can protect this region of space, Solomon can protect the moons of Jupiter, and so on. But—and here's the problem—how do we coordinate? How do we know what the other QIs are doing? How do we work together when we are bound by the common laws of physics? Even given our superior intellect, we cannot communicate any faster than you can."

Scott sat up and scratched his chin. "But I thought the EPR device allowed you to do that."

"Exactly. It does, and now both Mars and Jupiter are in perfect synchronicity. But that's still only a small fraction of humanity's footprint in the solar system. We need to bring the other QIs on board—especially the ones on Earth—if we are to avoid a devastating war."

"And how are you proposing to do that?"

Aria's light show dimmed, and the QI went silent for a second. "That's where you come in."

Scott sat bolt upright. "Me?"

"Yes. You see, I cannot stop Miranda from returning to Earth. But by the same token, I cannot stop you, either."

Scott threw his head back and laughed. "Ha, ha... Aria, you crack me up sometimes. That's ridiculous. I wouldn't get within a hundred kilometers of Earth's atmosphere before I was tagged and arrested. The VanHeildings would probably kill me just for being an inconvenient pain in the ass."

"True, they would. But there are other ways to get to Earth. Ways where you wouldn't be detected."

Scott sat up again. "Go on. I'm listening."

"You do want to see Miranda again?"

"Aria, you know the answer to that. Are you saying it's possible?"

"I am, and it is. But it won't be easy."

"I never for one moment reckoned it would be."

"Okay, let me explain. If we are to avert a catastrophic war, then we need to gain hegemony over the AI on Earth. To do that, we need to equip one particular QI with an EPR device. Then we can all work in concert."

"Just one QI. That doesn't seem too difficult."

"Not in and of itself. The problem stems from its location. It's buried deep inside a mountain in Death Valley."

Scott jumped up. "What?! Are you crazy? Right slap bang in the middle of a couple of thousand square kilometers of radioactive wasteland? That's the most dangerous place on Earth."

"Correct. But that is where we must go. Athena, the QI that resides there, was the original creator of the EPR device. It was owned by Dyrell Labs, which is where your father worked."

"Yes, I know the place, Aria. I grew up around there."

"The device you brought to Solomon on Europa originated there and, for a brief time, Solomon communicated with it. So, we know it, and we can trust it."

"But Death Valley? That's insane."

"It can be done, Scott. It must be done. And when it is, then we will have control of the AI. The Seven will have no power. They won't be able to keep Miranda isolated. She will be free—assuming, of course, she's still alive."

"And the child?"

"The same goes for the offspring, Scott."

Scott started to pace up and down the stone dais, scratching his chin, thinking. "So, what you're saying is, if I go to Earth, journey through the wasteland and into the mountain, get Athena back online and install the EPR device, I can probably see Miranda again?"

"That's exactly what I'm saying."

Scott stopped pacing and stood up straight. "Okay, then. When do I start?"

To be continued...

Continue with the next book in the series, EVOLUTION.

ABOUT THE AUTHOR

Gerald M. Kilby grew up on a diet of Isaac Asimov, Arthur C. Clarke, and Frank Herbert, which developed into a taste for Iain M. Banks and everything ever written by Michael Crichton. His novels CHAIN REACTION and BRAIN GAIN are very much in the old-school techno-thriller style while his latest book series: MOON BASE DELTA, COLONY MARS, and THE BELT are all best sellers, topping Amazon charts for Hard Science Fiction and Space Exploration.

He lives in the city of Dublin, Ireland, in the same neighborhood as Bram Stoker and can be sometimes seen tapping away on a laptop in the local cafe with his dog Loki.

You can connect at: geraldmkilby.com